## "Every man for himself..."

Katina rubbed her eyes and they at last came into focus. The boat was moving ahead steadily, with the

Russell, so she would go back to Homeplace. She would wait for Russell there.

He would know where to look for her.

Look for these historical romance titles
from Archway Paperbacks.

# The Great Chicago Fire
## 1871

### Elizabeth Massie

**AN ARCHWAY PAPERBACK**
Published by POCKET BOOKS
New York London Toronto Sydney Tokyo Singapore

AN ARCHWAY PAPERBACK *Original*

An Archway Paperback published by
POCKET BOOKS, a division of Simon & Schuster Inc.
1230 Avenue of the Americas, New York, NY 10020

Copyright © 1999 by Elizabeth Massie

ISBN: 0-671-03603-3

First Archway Paperback printing November 1999

10  9  8  7  6  5  4  3  2  1

AN ARCHWAY PAPERBACK and colophon are registered trademarks of Simon & Schuster Inc.

Cover art by Wendi Schneider

Printed in the U.S.A.

IL ages 15+

To some wonderful people in my life: all the members of Amnesty International Group #157 of Charlottesville, and in particular my great friend Meg West.

Also to Lisa Clancy, Peter Rubie, and Micol Ostow for making this book possible, to my mom Patricia Spilman for her love and support and creative inspiration, and to Andrew West for lending me some super research material!

# The Great
# Chicago Fire
## 1871

# 1

### Chief Williams Shares
### System, Pies, with Boston
### Fire Department Officials

Visitors from Boston, including fire department officials and city councilmen, arrived in Chicago yesterday afternoon for the purpose of examining the workings of our city's renovated fire alarm system. Boston Fire Department spokesman Leonard Brisco stated their business as gathering information on how they could improve their own systems at home.

"Our method for protecting the citizens of this fair city is the best in the country," Chief Fire Marshall Robert A. Williams told the Bostonians, describing the network which keeps the city informed and abreast of blazes in order to stop them before major damage can occur. "Not even New York can boast of a more proficient system for detecting and halting fires. The Queen of the West leads the way yet again. We have seventeen steam-driven fire engines, two hose elevators, four hook-and-ladder wagons, and twenty-three hose carts. I challenge you to find a more complete array in any American city!"

The entourage visited the Courthouse, where they were treated to a lunch of pork, breads, and rhubarb pie, supplied by Mrs. Williams and a friend, Mrs. Samuel Johnson. The visiting team was then escorted up the narrow steps of the one-hundred-foot-tall cupola, where Chicago watchmen faithfully scan the city twenty-four hours a day from the walkway outside the top of the tower.

"Each neighborhood has an alarm box mounted in a prominent place," Marshall Williams continued as the amazed Bostonians peered cautiously over the edge of the walkway, gazing out at the rooftops of Chicago, "usually on a storefront. These boxes are numbered, according to their location. If a fire is spotted by the neighborhood watch or by a common citizen, he telegraphs the Courthouse, using a number to designate the area of the city in which the fire was discovered. If the watchman in the tower spies smoke or flame, they likewise alert the fire houses in the vicinity of the fire. For added security, we also have the Courthouse bell, which is quite loud, and when it is rung, alerts the citizens of the danger of fire." For added emphasis, Marshall Williams had the watchman on duty ring the bell once, causing the visitors to cover their ears.

One Boston official, Jeffrey Van Osier, pointed out that he'd seen one of the alarm boxes on a stroll earlier, nailed to the outside of a barbershop, and was surprised to find it was locked. Marshall Williams explained simply that this prevented false alarms. "The keys to the boxes are kept by trustworthy citizens who live nearby."

After returning to the main floor of the Courthouse, Leonard Brisco asked, "Do you believe, then, that fire is no longer a threat to Chicago?"

To which Marshall Williams answered, "Fire will always be a concern. I would be a fool to think otherwise. But with our system of detecting and fighting blazes, I must say that we have never encountered a fire we could not control, and I cannot imagine that we will. The citizens of Chicago are in good hands, and can rest easy."

—George Rainey, *Chicago Tribune*,
June 2, 1871

\*　　　\*　　　\*

ELIZABETH MASSIE

The applause from the audience was greater than the size of audience warranted. With only sixteen people and their thirty-two hands, Katina Monroe would have thought the response to the final act of *Men and the Sky* would have barely been enough to stir the dust in the rafters or flicker the lights of the kerosene lanterns. But the men and women who had come to opening night and had dropped their meager donations into the jar by the door were thrilled with the story of two boys who grow up and, with the help of a magical bird, build a kingdom in the clouds. And now, as the four actors took their bows, some members of the audience called out, "Bravo! Bravo!"

Katina bowed deeply from the waist. Next to her, lanky Adam MacPherson, her fellow actor, bowed and whispered, "Author, author! You'll be our century's Shakespeare!"

"Hah!" Katina said softly. "I don't think the Bard and I have much in common, other than a love of words and fantasy. My stories are not poetic, but simple."

"Our audiences understand the simple," said Adam. "The rag collector, the knife grinder. They are the ones clapping, my friend!"

Katina glanced at him as she bent forward again and gave him a grin. Her heart pounded with the excitement of victory. *If moments like this could last forever,* she thought, *then I could forget the terrible things that have happened to me over the past years.*

After another few moments of bows, the other two

actors, Chadwick Tomms and Pip Harrison, stepped to the side of the stage, took the curtains—worn, paper-thin bed linens—and tugged them closed along the tight line of hemp rope. The applause began to fade. The actors grabbed each other in rough and cheerful hugs.

"Bravo, indeed!" said Chadwick, at twenty the oldest of the troupe. His sandy hair stood up, matted with sweat. "I can't believe I remembered all those lines."

"Aye," said curly-haired Pip, nineteen, his accent thick with the Scottish countryside from which he had come to Chicago five years earlier. "And I fed ya nearly a third of those lines from behind me hand. Yer brain is a sieve! Look on the floor there and I think that's where most of those forgotten lines ran down to!" Chadwick gave Pip a hearty shove, and they both laughed.

"Give the folks a few moments to clear the place," said Chadwick, shedding the woolen cape and tin crown that were part of his costume, "and we'll close up and go back to my flat. I've some stale gingerbread cake given me by Patterson and some ale to top it off. My mother works at the stockyard till midnight, so we'll have the place to ourselves for two hours."

"So be it!" said Adam.

"Cake it is!" said Pip.

Katina adjusted the black felt hat on her head and smiled but said nothing. She knew she wouldn't go to Chadwick's flat for talk and cake. It wouldn't be appropriate.

Suddenly two grinning faces appeared through the

curtains. Becky Alaimo, a skinny red-haired girl with a mangled ear, and Alice Montague, a chubby girl who would have been pretty had she not been missing four front teeth, giggled and invited the actors to come to their place of employment, the Stick Saloon on Quincy Street.

"Why don't you follow us back to work?" asked Alice, tossing her head so hard the red cap pinned to her straw-colored hair nearly flopped off. Her words hissed because of the missing teeth. "We're due there now. We've music, dancin', and entertainment! We'll even treat you to a free beer, first time."

Katina spoke quickly. "Thank you, but we have other plans, play notes and the like. Don't we, fellows?"

Becky's laugh was more like a bark. "Listen to the child! You's all such babies! Pity. Come on, Alice. They'll stop by when they grow up."

The girls' heads withdrew and their shrill laughter trailed them all the way out the stable door.

Chadwick rubbed at something in his eye. "We may not have play notes," he said. "But I'll be hanged before I'd step inside the Stick. They're as likely to rob you as entertain you. I'd rather take my chances on the streets."

Adam and Pip nodded in agreement.

There was not much to closing up the theater at the end of a show. Katina swept the stage and the wooden floor between the benches, shoving out the clumps of dried mud, while Pip returned the props to the prop box, Chadwick latched the windows, and Adam sat on the floor in what had once been a feed stall and sorted the coins from the donation jar by light of a lantern.

MacPherson Theater was a converted stable, owned by Adam's father, Sanford. Sanford had gone west to seek his fortune with his wife and the youngest seven MacPherson children, and Adam had promised to keep the stable in business. Three months after his family had gone, the stable was still in business, but there was not a horse nor a bit of tack in the place. Adam had cleaned it out, laid a wood floor, built a stage, constructed ten crude benches and sanded them down so a lady would not catch a splinter in her backside, then put the word out that he was going to produce plays. It had been in business now for almost a year.

Katina had met Adam at Anderson's Market on Fourth Avenue, where she ran errands and unloaded wagons. Adam shopped at Anderson's on Wednesdays, and when he had mentioned his new theater, Katina admitted she had written a play called *Fancy and the Captain*, about a silly young woman pining over a haughty sea captain. Adam asked to see it and was so impressed that it became the second production ever held in his theater. Katina quickly composed a second play in her hours after work, *Little Man of the Mountain*, a story of a forgetful gnome. This, too, had been performed on the stable's stage to the admiration of the residents of the destitute neighborhood.

The stable-turned-theater made no money compared to the stable as stable, but Adam loved performing so much it didn't matter. He earned his bread and butter as a carpenter's helper for a man named Simple Parker, mainly laying down planks for sidewalks in the business district of South Division just a few blocks northeast; Pip was employed at the gasworks on Monroe, and Chadwick manned the ovens at Patterson's bakery.

When the worst of the mud had been chased outside, Katina extinguished all but three lanterns and brought them back to the stall where Adam had been joined by Chadwick and Pip. The three were sitting in a circle, shirts off, wiping their chests.

"Just enough to pay for the kerosene for the next few Saturday nights and for each of us to have a few pennies," Adam told Katina as she sat down.

"Let's put our money together to have a new curtain sewn," said Pip.

"Ah, what this theater needs is a lady's touch," said Chadwick. "None of us can thread a needle. Our costumes are naught but our own clothes, decorated with a stray bit of tin or tassel!"

Adam shook his head. "A lady would only whine and complain that the theater is too shabby, the stage too rough, the kerosene too smoky. No, an all-man troupe is what I have and what I shall continue to have."

Katina crossed her arms. This conversation had come up before. There were always rips in costumes needing mending, or a female character who may have been more accurately played by a girl than a boy in girl's clothing. But Adam said keeping women out of his productions had not hurt William Shakespeare. Adam would never let a woman get involved with his theater. And as far as he knew, he had been true to his word. As far as he knew, there were no females in his theater troupe.

Adam hopped up and dropped the coins into the pocket of his trousers. He shoved one sleeve of his damp shirt into his waistband, then slipped his tattered wool jacket on over bare skin. "I'll concede one thing," he said. "When we've earned a good reputation and the rich have discovered our whereabouts, and when we are earning as much as the Steward Grand Theatre or Crosby's Opera House, then perhaps we shall hire a costume maker. But she would be paid to work and keep her thoughts to herself."

"Here, here!" said Chadwick. "To the time we are as well-respected as the Grand Theatre!"

The actors collected their lanterns and went outside. The June night air was beginning to mist over with an impending shower, and the road was rutted and muddy. Through the open windows of the four-story tenement across Fifth Avenue came the sounds of babies crying, men shouting, women yelling. From north and south along the road came other sounds—singing, fighting, a fiddle scratching out an unrecognizable tune, doors slamming. It was a usual Saturday night, with usual Saturday night noises.

Adam and Chadwick locked the stable door and then tugged it to make sure it was secured. There were child gangs and dangerous men who prowled the streets in this neighborhood, and one couldn't take chances without a lock. The gangs were out at all hours of the night, knocking folks senseless to steal watches, money, or anything else of interest. Although the people of this neighborhood had little worth stealing, that didn't matter to the thieves. During the day they worked alone in the fashionable business district several blocks over, picking the pockets of the gentlemen and ladies, but at night they would gather together, get drunk and angry, then turn their energies against their own people on their own streets.

"There," said Adam, turning from the locked door. "And now we're off to Chadwick's for refreshment."

"Except for me," said Katina.

They'd heard this before. "What is it with writers?" declared Pip. "Ye's been part of this acting troupe long as the rest of us, yet you've never gone out with us for a bit o' fun. Do ye dislike our company so much?"

"Do we bore you?" asked Chadwick. "Do we stink?"

Katina shook her head. "I'm tuckered is all. I would fall asleep with a mug in my hand and spill ale on Chadwick's mother's fine carpet."

"Fine carpet!" chuckled Chadwick. "Oh, that we have!"

"Come with us, please?" asked Adam.

"I need my sleep," said Katina. "Because tomorrow I shall begin writing yet another play, one even better than *Men and the Sky*."

Adam shook his head and squinted at her. It wasn't just poor light that made him do so. He had poor eyesight and was in great need of spectacles, which he could not afford. "Writers! A peculiar bunch if ever there was one. But remember we'll practice Thursday night. The play went well but there are always improvements that can be made."

Katina nodded. She could feel the first drops of rain plop onto her cap and run down the sides of her face. Her auburn hair, cut as short as Adam's and Chadwick's, was beginning to curl with the damp.

"You want us to walk you home?" asked Pip.

"I'll be fine," said Katina. "Robbers don't like the rain. They'll be finding shelter at a saloon or in the tunnels beneath the buildings of Conley's Patch till the worst is over."

"Suit yourself," said Adam. "Watch out for the road mud, though. I heard that after the rain last week, somebody down on Third Avenue found a brand-new hat lying on the street, only to pick it up and discover there was a man underneath. They asked the man wasn't he glad he'd been found? The man said yes, but the horse he was riding was still holding its breath!"

"Ah!" Katina laughed and swung her lantern, catching Adam in the back with it as the others moved off. "You had me believing for a moment!"

Holding her lantern out before her, Katina walked to the end of Fifth Avenue and turned west on Quincy by Sallee's Butcher Shop, watching her steps. The story of the man and the horse might be farce, but she had lost a shoe in the mud not long ago, and she had to pry it out with the thick, sturdy stick she kept in her back pocket for protection. But there was one consolation: she wore men's clothes, and they didn't require hands to clutch her skirts to keep her hems from dragging on the sorry surface of the street.

"William!" shouted Adam from the corner.

Katina turned around.

"You said earlier that you and the Bard have little in common. But think! You share a first name!"

"That we do," said Katina.

And the three other actors turned away, their lanterns bobbing, scattering shadows across the road and the side of a slowly passing wagon.

*William*, thought Katina. *That's me. Although I am eighteen-year-old Katina Monroe, no one in Chicago knows who I truly am. They all think I am fifteen-year-old William Monroe.*

The tenement in which she lived was two blocks up, down a narrow alley people referred to as Rat's Alley. Unlike the fancy mansions along Lake Michigan to the east, or the newer homes across the Chicago River to the north, this district was the bane of the city, rundown and dangerous. Katina hadn't known that when she had come here from Georgia. All she knew was that she needed a place she could afford, a place where she could forget the past eight years of her life.

The rain began to pick up. The steady patter soaked Katina's coat and trousers. She tried to walk faster, but the mud sucked at her shoes and made progress difficult. On both sides of the street, late-night gamblers and drinkers withdrew into their dimly lit shelters to continue their merrymaking. Others hid out in the cavernous, musky tunnels and makeshift rooms beneath buildings which had been raised as part of the city's ongoing renovation, but had not yet been filled in with soil or rock. Inside the Stick Saloon, someone was pounding out "Rain on the Lilacs" on a badly tuned piano.

Gritting her teeth, Katina hurried as best she could. At home, she would light the stove and dry her clothes. She didn't really plan on writing tonight. Her thoughts were fuzzy with fatigue. She just couldn't take a chance on spending extra time with her friends from the theater for fear they might discover her true identity. Although they were the closest friends she had, she didn't trust them completely.

Nobody could be trusted completely. It was a hard fact of life.

She reached the middle of the block and turned north into Rat's Alley. It was a narrow passage, lined with shanties and tall, rickety tenement buildings. Katina's boardinghouse was near the end, just past a pile of blackened beams that had been a garment factory before it burned in November. The residents of the alley had made the scorched hull a dumping ground for rubbish—rotten food, bones and gristle, splintered wood scraps, old paper, broken bottles. The place stank worse than the Chicago River, but at least on a rainy night the smell was reduced. Katina held her lantern higher, and the light splashed against the buildings on both sides of the street.

*A cup of tea will warm my mind and ease my stomach. What I wouldn't give to be able to have some of Chadwick's cake. How I miss good food, a comfortable house, clean clothes, someone to share my home and meals and conversation. How I miss family—*

Something hit her from behind, so hard that her lantern flew out of her hand and she fell facedown in the muddy road. Grit and gravel filled her mouth. "Owww!" she cried, instantly rolling over on her back to see what was after her.

Standing over her was a blond boy, no more than eight or nine, wielding a large metal pipe in his hand. He was dressed in knee pants, a coat way too large for him, and a smashed top hat.

"Give me what'cha got," said the child.

Katina had learned to fight here in Chicago, something she had never imagined she would do back in Georgia. In this city, however, it was a skill she had to have. *I should have let Adam walk me home,* she thought, reaching for the stick in her back pocket. *This boy would not have challenged the four of us!*

"I haven't anything," said Katina as she carefully pulled herself to her feet. Her back stung fiercely, but she would worry about that later. She held the stick behind her. She didn't want to strike him, or make him think she would. She knew these children; if they felt threatened they could become even more violent. The stick was a last resort. "Go on, or I'll call the authorities."

"Authorities!" said the boy. He spit in the road. "Authorities don't care to be here in Rat's Alley. Besides, the men here pay them to stay away! Now, empty your pockets or you'll have the end of this rod again!"

Katina knew getting away was better than a confrontation. She had learned to fight, yes, but she was not very skilled if surprise was not on her side. She slowly began to back up. On the road nearby lay her lantern, the globe cracked but not broken, sending a pool of light across the uneven ground. Several women, huddled beneath shawls, passed by on the other side of the road but didn't look her way.

"Go on," Katina said to the boy. "I've got nothing."

"You do!" said the boy. "I don't want to hit you again, but I will!" He took several steps forward, the pipe shaking in his grasp.

The burned hull of the old furniture factory was close. The boy might be younger, but Katina had longer legs. She could jump through the rubbish piles if lucky, and he would have to crawl over them. She could then kick a pile down on him and escape out the other side.

The boy waved the pipe at her face. "Give me!"

Katina spun about and made for the rubbish.

"Come back!"

She reached the rubbish and tried to stretch her legs enough to hurdle the pile, but her foot slipped in the mud and she crashed into it. Her cheeks were sliced by glass shards, and the palms of her hands were cut by exposed nails. The glass, splintered wood, and rotten food tumbled down around her shoulders. Her foot caught in a tangle of wire. Her protection stick was knocked from her hand and sent skittering away in the rain.

*He's going to hit me!* she thought, closing her eyes and raising her hands to protect her head. She gritted her teeth and prepared for the blow.

# 2

But the blow didn't come. She counted her breaths. *One, two, three, four, five.* She could hear a dog somewhere far down the alley, howling at real or imaginary prey. *Six, seven, eight. . . .*

She opened her eyes. Her heart continued to thunder.

*Nine. Ten?*

The boy was still in the middle of the road, and a tall man stood before him. The man was not easy to distinguish because of the rain and the night, but one hand pointed at the boy. The boy was looking down, the pipe still in his fist.

"Bruce," said the man at last. "What are you doing? You promised me."

The boy said nothing. He rubbed water from the bridge of his nose.

"Bruce!" the man said sharply.

"What?"

"Give me that pipe, and help me get that poor boy out of the rubbish."

The boy grunted but handed over the pipe. The man stuck it into the pocket of his long canvas coat, picked up Katina's cracked lantern, and took the boy by the shoulder. The boy grimaced but didn't pull away. Together they came up to where Katina was sprawled in the garbage, rain and trickles of blood running down her face.

The man handed the lantern to Katina. In its light she could see his face more clearly. He was not much older than she, perhaps nineteen or twenty. He was as tall as Adam, but much more striking, with longish brown hair and blue eyes shaded by heavy brows. His nose was straight and prominent. His voice was confident, bearing traces of an education most people in this neighborhood did not have. Katina felt her mouth go dry in embarrassment. She wished she had not met this handsome young man in this way.

"Are you hurt?" he asked. "Here." He held out his hand and Katina took it. With an easy move, he lifted her to her feet, where she stood wobbling slightly. The boy stared at his toes.

"You are hurt," said the man. "Ah, look at all this." He gently reached out and flicked pieces of glass from Katina's face. "The cuts aren't deep, though. That's good. Can you walk?"

Katina nodded.

"Bruce," said the man. "What should you do now besides stand there like a horse swishing away flies?"

The boy shrugged.

"Apologize," said the man.

"Sorry," said the boy.

"And offer to help me to show this boy to his home."

Bruce kicked at a pebble. "I don't want to."

"We had an understanding, Bruce," said the man. "Are you going to break your word to me?"

The boy slowly shook his head.

"Very well, then," said the man. Then he turned to Katina. His smile was kind and genuine. "My name is Russell Cosgrove. This is Master Bruce Charles. We are friends, and we look out for each other, don't we, Bruce?"

Bruce muttered, "Yes."

"And you are?" asked the man.

"William Monroe," said Katina, and the words raked her throat like the glass fragments had raked her flesh. If only she could tell Russell Cosgrove the truth. If only he could know that she was not a young boy at all but a young woman. She could not, of course. To destroy her disguise now would be to throw her entire life into a terrible spiral that she didn't want to consider.

Russell touched her face one last time, searching for glass, and then he let go. The warmth from his touch lingered on her cheeks as a blush. Surprised and embarrassed, she turned away so he wouldn't see.

"Master Monroe," said Russell. "Where do you live so we can escort you safely there?"

Katina stood as straight as she could. Her knees hurt. There was likely glass there, too, which she would remove at home. "The Brandermill Boarding House, over there. I was nearly home when Bruce attacked me. I don't need assistance, however. Just a promise from that young wolf there that he will leave unsuspecting folks alone."

"Are you certain?" asked Russell.

"Certainly I'm certain," said Katina. Her curious interest in this man was fading, to be replaced by growing anger. *Why is he being kind to this ruffian? The boy should be punished for such behavior! He should be locked up in a jail with all the other criminals who roam the streets at night.*

"Very well, then," said Russell Cosgrove. "Bruce, do you promise to leave other people alone?"

Bruce nodded.

"Then, good evening, Master Monroe," said Russell, giving a slight bow.

"Good evening," mumbled Katina. She turned on her heel and, ignoring the ache in her legs and back, snatched up her safety stick and strode with head held high to the steps of her boardinghouse. She did not look back until she was on the top step, and then only to take a quick peek. Russell Cosgrove and Bruce Charles were no longer in the rainy street.

Room 304 was on the third floor, up two flights of rickety steps and past many other flats, their doors locked against the nighttime. Mrs. Brandermill, the landlady, stuck her head out her door as Katina passed, her pretty, delicate face obscured in shadow. She whispered, "How did it go, William? How was the play? Oh, I wish I could have seen it!"

Katina smiled and said, "We were simply stupendous!"

Mrs. Brandermill nodded. "Someday I will come, just you wait. And I do look forward to it!"

Suddenly, Mr. Brandermill's furious, greasy-bearded face appeared above his wife's. Immediately, Mrs. Brandermill withdrew, and the man shouted after her, "Meg, get back in here 'fore I show you what's what!" And to Katina he growled, "Leave my wife alone, boy!"

Katina liked Mrs. Brandermill but hated her husband, John. Meg Brandermill was young, and pregnant with her first child. But John Brandermill was an old man, a gambler and a liar, and he treated his wife like an angry parent treated a child. The situation made Katina's blood boil.

Katina's flat was a single drafty room with a stove, a bed, a chair, and a window that looked west toward other tenements, grain elevators, and the South Branch of the Chicago River two blocks away. The stove and bed belonged to the Brandermills. Everything else, which was little indeed, belonged to Katina. A small stack of books, a little rectangular table that she'd bought from another tenant, a few cooking pots and utensils, and a scorched brocade satchel that had once been her mother's.

Katina locked her door, set the lantern on the table, and kicked off her shoes. Her stockings were soaked, as were her trousers and shirt and wool jacket, and they stank from the rubbish. She shed these and hung them to dry on nails that spotted the wall, then, naked, draped herself in a thin blanket and turned up the wick in the lantern. Unlike Chicago's fancier homes, this boardinghouse had no gas lighting or heat. The lantern was the only light she had; the stove the only heat.

She sat heavily on the sagging bed mattress and carefully picked the last of the glass bits from her knees. Then she wet a cloth from the water bowl on the table and dabbed her face, hands, and legs. She would be all right. The cuts stung, but none were bad enough to require bandages. She lay down, put her hands to her forehead, and stared at the ceiling.

She began to tremble. "I won't cry," she told herself aloud. "I won't cry. You've been through worse. Just don't think about it."

In the room above her, she could hear Mrs. Agee walking her baby. In the room next to her, she could hear Mr. Conlon talking his son out of a bad dream. There were good people in this dreadful neighborhood, many of them. It just seemed that so often the bad outweighed the good.

The lullaby drifted down from upstairs, made more tender by Mrs. Agee's soft Irish accent.

> *"Gingerbread, sugar cake, licorice, rose,*
> *Ten little fingers and ten little toes,*
> *Blue eyes, pink cheeks, bunting of silk,*
> *Dream thee child of honey and milk."*

This was the same lullaby Katina's mother had sung to her and to her sister so long ago.

So very long ago and far away.

Things had been good for Katina eight years ago. She had been ten years old and living at Merrifield, a large cotton plantation outside Atlanta, Georgia. Her parents, Samuel and Molly Monroe, took care of the business of farm and home, raising their two daughters, Katina and her younger sister Katherine, to be fine Southern ladies. There were riverside picnics, birthday parties, and recitals on the violin and flute. Katherine, eight years old, was Katina's best friend. They took arithmetic and penmanship lessons together under the strict eye of a dour, matronly tutor who came to Merrifield three days a week in her dour, matronly carriage. Katina made up plays, and she and her sister performed them, to the delight of their parents. Katina had imagined she would grow up, marry a handsome planter like her father, run the household, have several daughters, and write plays like *Our American Cousin*, which real actors would perform in real theaters for elegant audiences.

But then the war came.

Samuel Monroe left his family on his sorrel stallion, Old River, promising to return in a matter of months once the damn Yankees had decided it was best to leave the brave Confederates alone and not interfere with their secession.

Samuel Monroe had not come home. The damn Yankees had not left the brave Confederates alone but had ripped through Georgia with rifle, torch, and machete. General Sherman's men had plowed to the coast, destroying all in their path.

Afterward, Union renegades had fanned out and burned other places—for sport, it seemed. Merrifield had been looted and razed. The slaves had been set off, the cattle and horses strung together to be taken, and what crops couldn't be stripped and crammed into saddle bags and feed sacks were hacked to pieces in the fields.

Katina had been writing a skit down by the stream when the renegades came. When she realized what was happening, she climbed up a large oak tree to hide. She watched with horror as the stable, barns, and house were set afire. Even to this day, she could hear the cries of her mother and sister as they'd been left to die in the blazing house.

*And you did nothing, Katina.*

Katina rolled onto her side and looked out the small window of her flat. All she could see was rivulets of rain on the window glass and distorted lamplight from the windows of the tenement building behind her own. She did not want to remember what had happened in Georgia, but she did. The memories were living spirits, coming back and tormenting her when she was exhausted or lonely, and least able to deal with them.

The renegades had at last left the plantation for the road, passing beneath the tree where she hid, trembling. She remembered seeing her paper and pen in the grass beneath her and being certain the men would see them, too, and would look up to find her there. She remembered her heartbeats, so loud in her temples and so frantic in her chest that it seemed a miracle that the soldiers couldn't hear them as well. She remembered the laughter of the men as they mentioned General Sherman and how they were faring much better since leaving "the Old Bear," and how they would soon be rich men thanks to the ignorant Southern farmers who dared leave their wives and riches behind to fight for states' rights. Katina had bit her tongue hard so as not to scream, and she had not.

She did not scream as she clung to the scabby branch of the oak and watched the house, blackened and smoldering, fall in on itself. She did not scream after she had picked through the rubble of Merrifield, finding nothing recognizable but a scorched satchel that had belonged to her mother. She wandered the road, heading west, not wanting to go north for fear of the Yankees, not wanting to go south for fear of finding more destruction. Her mind, numbed with shock, kept her from feeling the hunger, the fear, the weariness.

Two days later she was picked up by a pious young couple in a wagon who took her to an orphan asylum sponsored by their parish. Willowbrook, once an elegant boarding school for girls, was now a home for destitute orphans, many made so by the war. The old house was not a victim of the war but of age and disrepair. The poorly shingled attic collected rainwater during storms, and the water leaked onto the girls and boys as they tried to sleep in their cots at night. The cellar, where the garden's yield of potatoes, apples, and onions were stored, was the nesting ground for mice and black widows.

Miss Althea Innis, the matron of Willowbrook, did not offer the kind of lessons that Katina had had at Merrifield. Instead, the boys and girls of the asylum learned domestic chores—cleaning, cooking, baking, sewing, weaving, mending, gardening, animal husbandry—all to the tune of Miss Innis's Bible verses and leather riding crop.

Young girls fared worse under Miss Innis's eye than boys. The boys were allowed to take the asylum's wagons to nearby farms to sell the vegetables, eggs, and milk. Miss Innis did not strike the boys as severely as she did the girls, and she often chastised the girls with her grim predictions.

"Ah," the old woman would say. "Boys shall grow up and find their way. God made boys to be independent. But you, girls, you've naught to look forward to but a life under the discipline of husband or master. Get used to the pain and position of your gender."

Boys didn't stay at Willowbrook as long as the girls did; with Miss Innis's help, most of them found jobs or at least the courage to go out on their own by the time they were fifteen. For five years, Katina lived at Willowbrook, bleakly counting the days until she turned eighteen and would be put out or took up a position as a teacher at the institution, as several other girls had done.

But then, on a night in mid-December, 1869, Katina had discovered something that gave her a plan and a flicker of hope. Inside the scorched satchel she'd rescued from Merrifield, she had found a pocket within a pocket, and inside that, a short note on a single, age-faded sheet of paper. The return address had been Chicago.

The wind outside Katina's flat shifted, throwing the rain hard against the window glass. Katina wrapped her arms over her face, fighting to keep tears at bay. Willowbrook and Miss Innis were in the past. She did not want to remember, but there was nothing she could do to keep the memories away.

She had run away from Willowbrook. Late at night, when the frosty December moon was full and the sky was speckled with indifferent stars, she had slipped from her bedroom window with the satchel. Behind the old mansion, she'd yanked boy's clothing from the clothesline, stuffed the satchel full of apples and pears from the root cellar, climbed over the stone wall, and took the road north. She wasn't sure how far Chicago was, but it didn't matter. She would find it. She was no longer a little orphan girl, she was almost seventeen. It was time to determine her own fate, no matter how frightening that prospect seemed. An address from a city in the northwest could be her salvation.

*Mrs. Bradford Monroe, 1345 S. Michigan Avenue, Chicago, Illinois.*

Several miles up the road, as it had begun to sleet, Katina had hidden beneath a bridge and changed into the trousers, shirt, and jacket. Miss Innis always said boys could go places girls could not. Boys were not harassed because of their frailty. Katina did not feel frail that night; beneath a sheen of sweat and anxiety, she felt strong. But being thought of as a boy would make traveling easier. She would keep her disguise until she was safe by the warm hearth in the house on Michigan Avenue.

But Chicago was more dangerous than any rural road in the South, and the family living at 1345 South Michigan Avenue had refused to see her. The burly family maid had chased Katina away from the gate, hurling stones and shouting, "Poor folks always lyin' to get a little somethin' what ain't theirs! Be gone, tramp!" Bruised and shaking, Katina found a room to rent in a boardinghouse in Rat's Alley. She continued to dress as a boy, named herself William, and got a job selling *Tribune*s on snowy street corners. *It won't last long, this disguise*, she told herself. *I'll get past that dreadful maid and convince Mr. and Mrs. Bradford Monroe that we are related. Then I can be myself once more. A girl of good station and refined nature.*

Every day for the first two weeks, she trudged the snowy streets to Michigan Avenue to present herself, Katina Monroe, to the people in the elegant home. And every day, the maid would catch her outside the gate and threaten to beat her if she did not go away.

"But I've this letter!" she said time and again. "My family was killed in the war, but I am alive! I'm Katina Monroe! Don't you know me?"

It did not matter. She was not allowed on the property. She spent her seventeenth birthday, February fifteenth, alone in her drafty room in Brandermill Boarding House, stuffing rags into wall cracks to keep the rats from coming in to share her mattress.

"Enough!" Katina told herself, sitting up abruptly on her bed and clenching her fists. "Nothing will change the past. Only the future can be altered. Now get some sleep, Katina. You've got a letter to deliver in the morning."

She blew out the lantern, curled up on the bed, and closed her eyes. At long last, sleep came, and her dreams were of rain and renegades and laughter and fire.

# 3

Russell Cosgrove's home was on the corner of Adams Street and Fifth Avenue, in a sagging two-room apartment over the butcher shop belonging to Lieutenant and Olive Sallee. The Sallees had their quarters in a long, narrow room behind the shop where the meat—sometimes fresh and sometimes rancid—was delivered on Tuesdays and Fridays. Tonight, Lieutenant and Olive were arguing down in the shop, loud enough that Russell could hear Lieutenant accusing Olive of spending too much time visiting her sister and Olive accusing Lieutenant of leaving the back door open long enough for a dog to come inside and run off with a link of sausages.

"Those two have voices shrill enough to shred wallpaper," Russell muttered to himself as he closed the door against the rain. He shed his coat and went through the small front room and into the bedroom, where he poured water from an enameled tin pitcher into a washbasin, and splashed his face with cold water.

It was after midnight, and Russell was exhausted. His feet throbbed from hours of walking and standing, yet the day had been particularly fruitless. He'd spent most of the morning at the office of the *Chicago Tribune* in the city's bustling business district, leaning against a post in the front hall, waiting to speak to a reporter—any reporter—but getting nothing but dour looks from the employees who came and went. He had a story they needed to write, a story the people of the city needed to read, but no one seemed to want it.

"I'm sorry, *sir,*" the woman at the front desk had said in a sarcastic tone after he explained his presence for the tenth time, "your so-called *story* would not be of interest to our basic readership. If you want it told, perhaps you should find a printing press of your own." He had left the office after wasting four hours.

*I'll get a reporter's attention some way,* Russell thought. He wiped his face with a tattered towel, then sat down at the tiny desk in the corner of the room and turned up the wick on the lantern. A yellow glow fell over the surface of the desk and across the backs of his chapped hands. He opened his journal, dipped his pen into the well of ink, and began to write an account of the night's confrontation.

"I was on the streets tonight," he wrote. "A rainy night it was, and dark as hell. In Rat's Alley I found Bruce, who had struck an older boy in the back. What do I do about Bruce? After all the time I've spent talking to him, being a friend, sharing meals, thinking I'd convinced him that violence is not an answer, he is still wild."

Russell lifted the pen and looked at what he had written. He had pages and pages of such entries. Every evening since moving into this flat four weeks ago, he'd kept records of all he had witnessed. He had come to the worst part of town on purpose, to observe, to record. To help.

Russell slammed the pen on the desk and ran his hands through his soaked hair. Bruce had been a terrible disappointment. And there were many other children just like him, and men and women, without hope, without education, without even a sense of safety on their own streets, angry and defensive, unable to see anything beyond the present moment. It was his plan to do something about it, but the puzzle of despair was too much for one person to solve. How could one man accomplish what had to be done? *I need help, but who is there to help me?*

He put his head down on his desk. The rush of the rain outside made him feel more tired. His arm hurt where he'd been cut three nights earlier. He'd been visiting dance halls and saloons, begging for donations to share with the poor, knowing that the people who ran these places were the only ones in the neighborhood with money. Until he could get the attention of Chicago's wealthy, he had to go somewhere. But the saloon owners had laughed him out to the road, saying they had enough to deal with their own worries without adding those of their neighbors.

"You want me to donate to the poor?" one bad-breathed proprietor had barked in Russell's face after a drunk had slashed Russell in the forearm with a dagger and held him at bay at knifepoint. "Why should I give away anything I worked so bloody hard for? Take your charity requests to the church!"

And so Russell had bandaged his arm, toughened his resolve, and taken his requests to the church. Seven of them shut their doors in his face, explaining that they performed enough charity as it was by ministering to the souls of the destitute. "It is God's plan that there always be poor," explained one stiff-necked minister named Botkins. "It is a judgment on them and their immoral behavior. Leave it be."

*I will not leave it be*, Russell thought angrily. *I will never let it be.*

There was a letter between the pages of the Bible on the desk, and Russell pulled it out and held it up to the lantern light. The envelope was worn from much handling. The sweat-softened note inside, dated two weeks earlier, was from a friend he'd known at Brickmeyer's School, the college he'd attended in northern Chicago before he'd quit and moved to Chicago's poorest slum.

"My dear Russell," the letter began. "I've no idea where you are, but I thought that if I got this letter to your parents they might be kind enough to pass it on to you. How are you? I was dismayed to discover that you have quit Brickmeyer's, disappearing before our very eyes! Such promise you showed, too, in your law studies. Where are you now? New York City? Boston? Or have you decided to take a train across the western plains to search for gold?

"I miss you so very much. Please tell me you left for a good reason, such as the temptation of gold, and not because we were falling in love.

"If this letter finds its way to you, please reply. I have one more year of studies here, and then I plan on opening my own school to educate young ladies. I have the means to open my school wherever I wish, and would not hesitate to follow you where you have gone. I miss you.

"Yours always, Rebecca."

Russell ran his thumb over the signature, then slipped the note back into the Bible. He leaned back and stared out his window at the rain. Rebecca Molloy was a beautiful girl, with hair the color of wheat and eyes as green as Irish shamrocks. She was a year younger than he, and like him, had attended Brickmeyer's College on St. Claire Street. Russell, who had been born and raised in the working-class West Side, had saved his money from his work on a grain elevator and enrolled at Brickmeyer's at seventeen to study to become a lawyer. Rebecca Molloy, because of her father's standing in the community and friendship with the headmaster of the school, had been admitted to study whatever subjects caught her fancy. She was also allowed to have a female chum enroll, as well, so she wouldn't be the only woman in attendance. She chose Candace Stephenson, a quiet redhead.

Russell had worked hard the two years he attended Brickmeyer's, absorbing mathematics, law, and, particularly, philosophy and theology. Rebecca had attended an astronomy class with Russell, and they had become friends. She was smarter than most of the young men at Brickmeyer's. She and Russell spent many hours discussing new medical discoveries, literature, and Russell's evolving ideas about individual liberty versus collective traditions.

"When one loses his freedom for anything short of criminality, it cannot be rationalized that it is for the common good," he had said as they'd sat in the school's side garden in the fall. "Look at the institute of slavery, and how it corrupted all involved. No, we as a society owe it to ourselves to protect even the most lowly. It is the only way to keep our honor and our moral dignity intact."

"Yet even criminality is constantly redefined," Rebecca had said as the leaves from a poplar tree cast swirling shadows on her pretty face. "Some consider it a crime to be poor or uneducated."

"True," said Russell. "Some respected religions promote such ideas. But they are wrong. All people are equal, without qualification. Injustice cannot parade as morality, and if I must develop my own theology to be true to what God has put in my heart, I shall do it."

"What would your parents say to such a declaration?"

"I would hope they would say 'Godspeed.' "

"Indeed," said Rebecca.

That was when Russell, surprising himself, had leaned over and given Rebecca a kiss on the cheek. He had then confided in her that he was from a poor family on De Koven Street. He had explained that his grandfather had been a Potawatomi warrior—a fact that most well-to-do Chicagoans would have recoiled against—and that the Potawatomis had been forced by government agents to sell their land in 1835 around the village of Chicago so the city could grow. His family understood what it was like to be taken advantage of by the powerful. Rebecca seemed neither offended nor shocked. She merely linked her arm in his and said she was glad they were becoming close.

Rebecca invited Russell to visit her home in mid-April. Russell did not have enough money for another semester, and Rebecca assured him that her parents would be happy to find a way to help him continue.

The trip to her home was an uncomfortable one for Russell. He had never asked for anything from anybody, but if Rebecca's parents were willing to give him the chance to finish his schooling, then he would have to swallow his pride.

The Molloys lived on the North Side, near Lincoln Park, in a large brick house. The opulence of the house made him uneasy, and the snobbery of Rebecca's parents surprised and angered him. Rebecca's mother assured Russell that the Molloy family were not common Irish immigrants, such as one would find in the Bohemian shacks on the West Side, alongside the Germans, the Italians, and the Scandinavians. The Molloys had been wealthy in Ireland and were wealthy still. Mr. Molloy made his money as a merchant, and Mrs. Molloy confided with a smug grin that her home boasted more finery than did her neighbors'.

Russell had sat on the overstuffed chair in the parlor, holding his teacup in his lap, feeling claustrophobic amid the clutter of crystal, porcelain, silver, and lace. It was obvious Rebecca had not told her parents that Russell Cosgrove was a poor boy from the West Side, that his own family lived in a single-room cottage with a milk cow, and that he had Indian blood in his veins.

After the visit, Russell had bid a barely controlled farewell, then had gone out to the street and yelled. Rebecca scurried after him, apologizing, but at that moment, Russell thought he saw in her eyes a glint of the superiority that had blazed in her mother's. If she had truly cared for him, she would have told her parents the truth about him. Perhaps she had merely found his controversial thoughts entertaining. He realized he could not continue to go to Brickmeyer's and talk about improving social conditions. He had to work for them. He couldn't afford more college, and he might never be a lawyer, but it didn't take a degree in law to make a difference.

As Rebecca stood by the road, Russell had bid her farewell and strode away, never to see her again. He had not returned to school nor to his parents' house on De Koven. He took the little remaining money he'd saved and sought out the most destitute area of the city. An apartment over a butcher shop was all he needed.

He spent the next days eating from rubbish dumps, drinking from rain barrels and burst water mains, and praying for guidance.

*Here is the problem, and here are two hands. What am I to do?*

The answer came the following morning, while Russell was walking through a filthy alley near Conley's Patch. He found a family of feral cats beneath an empty house, and as he knelt to coax them out, he spied a boy there as well. The boy snarled at Russell and scampered back into the darkness, but Russell knew the boy was alone and had no safe place to be.

It was Russell's duty, then, to find a place for people who needed it, a safe, clean place to come for food and education. It was his job to alert the rich to the plight of the poor and to convince them that it was their moral duty to help. The boy beneath the house had been Bruce Charles, and with daily determination, Russell had befriended the boy and tried to teach him about civility.

Russell looked up at the ceiling. He could see a fat black spider in the corner, working frantically to build a web with its gossamer strands of silk. "I need just two things," he said to himself, to the spider, to God. "A small building to start with, to use as a haven for those who need it, and a writer who will take my simple words and make them into a story that will grip this city by the heart."

The spider paused, as if considering the statement, then returned to its spinning in the dark, dusty corner.

# 4

❦

## Progress Continues in the Raising of the City; Two Workmen Injured

The effort which began in our fair city in 1856 continues, that of raising the many municipal buildings above the mud and resurfacing the ground with stone and packed earth. As any citizen of Chicago knows, one of the major problems here is the mud. Due to this concern and with thanks to those gentlemen with foresight and an understanding of construction and engineering, many buildings have already been hoisted up off the soggy land by means of crank-operated jackscrews and set on stilts when they have reached the desired height. While a good number of buildings have not yet been filled in underneath, sometimes making wind a greater trouble than usual as it blows though the stilts and out to the pedestrians on the streets, progress continues, and it has been projected that completion of the raising project may come as soon as two years from now.

Monday morning, while hoisting West's Print Shop and Apothecary, two workmen caught their hands in the jackscrew, which crushed the fingers of one and amputated the hand of the other. The crew's overseer explained that the men had been drinking the night before and had been unduly thoughtless in their work. The man who had lost his hand, Herman Strinstein, told this reporter that he was not a drunk, that he had been careful, but the overseer had been rushing to get the job done so they could move on to the next building by the end of the week.

"I gave my hand for this," Strinstein complained from his bed at Central Hospital. "For the great wooden city, like a slave in Egypt! Now how shall I feed my family? I should like to go home to Germany if I had the means."

—George Rainey, *Chicago Tribune*,
June 4, 1871

When Katina went outside to the alley late Sunday morning, the rain had slowed to a drizzle. The air was thick with the smell of worms and dead mice. She pulled the brim of her cap down to keep it from blowing away and thought, *I wish never to feel another rain-*

*drop. How much water can one city tolerate? We've got a whole lake, that should be plenty.* A passing wagon full of potatoes splashed the bottoms of her trousers, but she just shifted the satchel she clutched from one hand to the other and began walking. She was on her way to Michigan Avenue. She had a letter to deliver.

It did not take long to leave the shanties, saloons, and dance halls behind. The business section of the city was only three blocks to the northwest, and here was another world, an elegant world. Roads were wide, paved with pine blocks or cobblestones to help alleviate the problems of winter mud and summer dust. Trees, covered with the thick, green leaves of June, lined the streets. Gaslights on wrought-iron posts stood on corners and at intervals along the street. Fire hydrants were new and made of cast iron, unlike the wooden, churnlike ones in the slum. Horsecars traveled along steel tracks in the road surfaces. Carriages and tea carts clattered up and down the streets, carrying well-dressed occupants on their way to church. Women strolling with their husbands wore satin and velvet gowns with proper bustles in the back. Men wore black waistcoats and long jackets, with gloves, hats, and walking canes.

Although Chicago was a city built primarily of fine Illinois and Wisconsin wood, some of the buildings in the business district were painted to look like marble or stone. Signs on doors and awnings made it clear that the establishments' clientele were of the upper class. "Suits for the Discriminating Gentleman," "Alice Morrison's Ladies' Boutique," "Arthur and Williamson, Attorneys at Law." Very different from

"The Stick Saloon" on Quincy and "Raymond Atlinger, Ragseller" in Rat's Alley. Even the birds who circled the air around the Steward Grand Theatre and pecked at the front steps of Crosby's Opera House seemed haughtier than slum birds. A pair of them squawked at Katina from a light pole as she paused to pick a rock from her shoe. She threw the rock at them and they flew away.

Inside Katina's satchel were the only pieces of women's clothing she owned, a white blouse and a blue skirt with white piping on the hem, the ones she had worn when she had escaped from Willowbrook. She had grown over an inch taller between her seventeenth and eighteenth birthdays, and so she'd had to buy a rag from Raymond Atlinger to sew around the hem to bring the skirt back to a decent length.

As was true for most streets in the city, there were wide, wooden sidewalks on both sides of these avenues, in some places three to five feet off the ground. This way, pedestrians could move more easily from business to business, away from the traffic and mud in the street. Chicago had been built on swampy land. Katina strolled along the sidewalk, peering into shop windows as she passed. She saw her reflection in beveled-edged window glass, and it was a sad sight, indeed. No longer pretty and trusting, she was now scraggly and steely-eyed.

*But I remember how to be polite,* she thought as she moved from the window. *If I get to talk to them, I'll make up for my appearance with actions. Mother used to say, "Pretty is as pretty does."*

Soon she saw a slice of Lake Michigan through the buildings, and it was only minutes before she found herself on a cobblestoned residential street lined with refined houses faced in brick or wood shingles. Large yards were filled with azaleas and rose of Sharon, and flowerbeds had been newly dug for springtime bulbs. Front porches were furnished with wicker chairs and potted evergreens. The lake shimmered, its small waves rising and falling like the heartbeat of a gentle giant. Sailboats, steamboats, and barges rode the water, carrying goods from the city to destinations far away.

The Monroe house was three stories tall, built of stone and surrounded by a matching stone wall. Standing on tiptoe, Katina could peer over the wall at the well-tended lawn. There was a whitewashed gazebo, a fishpond, and a cobblestone path through a geometric planting of boxwood. An air of prosperity hung about the property.

*I belong there,* Katina thought. *They are family, and I am as well-bred as they. I'll make them understand.*

Behind a thick holly bush that hugged the exterior of the stone wall, Katina pulled her skirt on over her trousers, then shoved the trousers into the satchel. She exchanged her cap for a scarf she'd bought several months ago and wrapped her short, damp hair as fashionably as she could without a mirror. She was sure she looked like a washerwoman, but at least she looked like a woman.

"Perhaps today is the day," she whispered, taking the note from the satchel. She lifted her head, straightened her shoulders, and walked around the wall to the front gate.

Every other Sunday, Katina visited this house by the lake. After the first, frustrating weeks, during which she believed the family would recognize her and take her in, and after shouting at them from behind the gate, clutching the bars and shaking them as if she would pull them out, she realized that her persistence and dignity would have to overcome their fear and stubbornness. If she slept outside their house or continued to shout at them, they would have the authorities cart her off to an insane asylum. If she climbed over the wall to confront them, they would have the authorities cart her off to jail. And so, she calmly brought a note to the house every other Sunday, dressed as best she could on the chance that she might indeed come face to face with one of the family members. She pulled the chain of the brass bell at the top of the gate and waited.

As the raindrops fell and dampened her scarf, she stood and watched for a face to peek from between a pair of downstairs curtains or through the ribs of upstairs blinds. Often she would catch glimpses of the Monroe family. There was a father, thin and light-haired, and a mother, pudgy and with dark hair. And there was a daughter, with hair always piled on her head in curls and adorned with red ribbons. The girl was young, perhaps twelve or thirteen. Who was this girl to Katina? A second cousin? A niece, perhaps? Why had Katina never heard of the Monroes of Chicago, back when she lived at Merrifield? She had wondered this often.

The family in the stone house would often glance out after she rang the bell at the gate, then shake their heads and draw back into the shadows of their home. No one would come out to meet Katina, but they knew she was there, and they knew the note was there. A note that repeated the same information over and over again, a note that maybe, someday, would make them realize who it was that stood beyond the gate.

Today the maid came out to the porch at the sound of the bell and shooed Katina with a clap of her hands and the words, "Leave us alone, you!"

Across the distance of the yard, Katina looked the maid in the eye. She didn't know what happened to her notes. Maybe the maid threw them all away and the family never read them at all. But there was nothing else to do but to keep trying. Katina had made a life for herself in Rat's Alley, but if she thought it would never get any better, she knew she would go mad.

"On, now!" shouted the maid.

Katina held up the note, and then slipped it through the bars of the gate. It fluttered to the walkway and landed in a puddle.

"Now!" shouted the maid.

Katina turned away, and walked back to the holly bush, where she gritted her teeth against the sting of disappointment, then pulled out her trousers and became William once more.

The walk back to her boardinghouse always felt much longer than the walk to Michigan Avenue. As the lake disappeared behind her amid the tall buildings, she felt as if she were being swallowed alive, sucked back into a great monster whose belly was Rat's Alley. The bustle in the streets—the argument of men beside an overturned fish cart, the laughter of children in a churchyard, the braying of an impatient mule, the clanging of the courthouse fire bell telling the city that something, somewhere, was burning—all these sounds tangled in her ears. The satchel grew heavy, and she had to force one foot in front of the other.

On the sagging stoop outside the entrance to the Stick Saloon on Quincy Street, Alice Montague and Becky Alaimo sat with parasols over their heads, looking glum. Their frilly red dresses seemed wilted.

"Good morning, William," Becky said as Katina passed. "You're a wet, dreadful sight."

"I could offer the same compliment," said Katina. "Why are you sitting outside?"

"Oh," said Alice, "Madame Jocelyn is in a snit. She is actin' crazy, throwin' chairs and cussin'. There is hardly a customer now, so we thought it was best to be out of the way till she was done."

"She get in a snit often?" Katina asked.

Alice nodded. "I think she's gettin' meaner with old age. I tell you, ain't a meaner saloon owner 'round here than Madame Jocelyn. But what can we do? Can't quit. I ain't never worked nowhere but a saloon before."

"Yes," said Becky. "She pays us, we put up with it."

There was a sudden scream from up the street. Katina glanced up and saw a woman on the corner, flailing her arms and yelling at the top of her lungs. A man was trying to grab her. Katina squinted and recognized the woman as her landlady, Meg Brandermill. And there was blood all over the front of her dress.

"Mrs. Brandermill!" Katina cried. She left Alice and Becky and ran up the street, trying not to trip in the ruts or mud. When she reached the corner she slammed the heels of her hands against the man's back, sending him to the ground with a grunt. "Leave her alone!" Katina shouted. "Get away from her!"

"God help me!" Mrs. Brandermill cried, her hands holding her face. Her fingers were covered with blood.

The man rolled over and scrambled to his feet, and as he did, Katina turned with her safety stick in her hand. "Don't touch her," she hissed.

It was then she recognized Russell Cosgrove. He didn't look as composed as he had the night before, with his hair knocked in all directions, and his hands held up as if he thought she would, indeed, hit him. "Wait," he panted. "I was only trying to help!"

Katina's mouth opened in her confusion.

"Ohh," moaned Mrs. Brandermill, leaning over and holding her knees. "Oh, why? God have mercy on me!"

"I was trying to help, William," said Russell. "Now help me help her or get out of the way!"

"All right," Katina said, her voice emptied of its fury. She pocketed her safety stick, turned to Mrs. Brandermill, and both she and Russell held out their hands to try to steady the woman. The woman seemed mad with pain. "Mrs. Brandermill, it's William!" said Katina. "Please let us take you home. You are terribly hurt!"

"I can't go home!" Mrs. Brandermill wept, her head hanging down and her words coming in great whoops. Katina could see blood on the side of her bonnet, and a great gash in Mrs. Brandermill's cheek.

"What happened, ma'am?" asked Russell.

"Men wouldn't understand. It's a woman's plight!"

"Oh, we would," insisted Katina. "We can take you to a doctor, if you'd rather. Just tell us what is wrong so we can assist you!"

"I haven't got money for a doctor!"

"That doesn't matter," said Russell. He was stooped down now, trying to look up at the woman's face. "Let us take you. We can worry about payment later."

"No! Oh, you just . . . you . . ." said Mrs. Brandermill. And then she gasped and fainted, dropping to the roadside like a sack of turnips.

"Help me!" said Russell, giving Katina a quick glance. "I haven't got money for a doctor, either, but St. Andrew's is close, and a church will certainly help us find a charitable physician. But we must be quick!"

Katina took Mrs. Brandermill's arms and Russell took her ankles and they lifted her, barely, off the street. The woman was small, but her pregnancy had given her extra weight that Katina knew was too much for her to lift. But then, standing beside them, were Becky and Alice, their hands to their mouths and their eyes huge. "We heard her all the way down at the Stick," said Alice. "Will she die?"

"We'll do all we can to keep her from it," said Russell.

And so the four of them lifted and carried Mrs. Brandermill a full two and a half blocks, to the door of St. Andrew's Church, and then up the wooden steps and into the dark, candle-lit sanctuary.

They lay the woman in the aisle, and while Alice and Becky knelt beside her and patted her hand, Katina and Russell ran in search of the pastor.

"Hello? Someone, quickly!" called Katina. "We have an injured woman. Please!" Her voice echoed in the deep recesses of the dark church. She'd not been inside a church since leaving the orphan asylum, and being in one now made her uncomfortable, as if God wouldn't remember who she was.

"Hello?" shouted Russell. "Pastor Botkins?"

Katina tried a door to one side of the altar, but it was locked. Russell went to the second one and reached for the knob. At that moment a portly, bald man in black garb came out. He was frowning and wiping crumbs from his mouth. "What is this commotion in my church?" he demanded. "What are you all about here?"

Russell took the man firmly by the elbow and turned him so he could see down the aisle. "We've a hurt woman in need of immediate attention. Have you knowledge of a charitable physician who will attend her?"

Pastor Botkins made a grunting noise and rolled his eyes. "Another one," he mumbled.

"Another one what?" asked Katina.

"Another one who's losing a baby, can't you see? The blood, the way she's cramped up? Let her lose it.

God knows we have enough living in this slum as it is. The mother won't die. They hardly ever do."

Russell grabbed the man by the shoulders and shook him. Russell's eyes blazed. "*God* knows? God knows no such thing! How dare you!"

"And it's more than losing a baby!" said Katina. "She's been beaten, badly!"

"Get her out of my sanctuary," said Pastor Botkins. He jerked from Russell's grasp and shook a threatening finger at the man. "Now, before I have you thrown out. All that bloody mess is spoiling the runner on the floor."

Russell gave an exasperated cry and threw up his hands. "Your sanctuary? You pious pig! God forgive you and your deadly arrogance! William, let's go elsewhere!"

On the runner in the aisle, Mrs. Brandermill had begun to writhe in pain, her feet kicking at the floor and her teeth gnashing at the air. Her dress was completely drenched in blood now. "Oh," said Alice, no longer trying to comfort the woman but flat back against a pew, shaking visibly. "She's gonna die, I can smell it!"

"No!" said Russell. "We can't let her die, we . . ."

But Becky said, "She gonna die, sir. She got but a second, and if we move her, her last moment on earth here will be nothing but jostlin' on top of the pain."

Katina looked toward the altar. Pastor Botkins had vanished, most likely to return to his lunch. She looked back at Mrs. Brandermill. "Who beat you? Was it John?"

"It don't matter now," said Alice, shaking her head. "Knowing who beat her won't keep her from dying."

"But it *does* matter!" insisted Katina.

Slowly, Mrs. Brandermill nodded.

"It was John?" pressed Katina. Mrs. Brandermill nodded.

"It don't matter!" said Alice. "Let her alone!"

The four stared at the woman on the floor. And then, Becky said, "Rest her, she's gone."

And Mrs. Brandermill was, indeed, gone. With a quiet sigh, her head rolled over to rest on Pastor Botkins's runner. Her shoes stopped digging at the floor. Her eyes, half open, no longer blinked. The sweet landlady was dead.

# 5

"Sweet Jesus," whispered Becky. "She's gone."

Alice crossed herself and kissed her knuckle.

Russell lifted the dead woman and held her, saying through clenched teeth, "This should not happen."

Katina stared, not believing her kind young landlady was no longer alive, nor was the baby she had so desired. Mr. Brandermill should be arrested! He should face judgment with jury and judge! But Katina's mouth was so dry she could not speak. Furious tears welled in her eyes but she dug them away.

The four stayed there for what seemed like a very long time before they at last lifted the dead woman and carried her to the undertaker's shop on Jackson Street. The undertaker, a scarecrowish man covered in sawdust from the coffins he built, brushed his hands off and demanded to know who was going to pay for the burial. "I don't work for folks who haven't paid! I got to make a living, even if I make it off the dead!"

"I will get the money to you in the morning," said Russell without hesitation. Then the undertaker scribbled a bill for coffin and burial at the paupers' plot near the South Branch of the river and handed it to Russell.

Becky and Alice left for the Stick Saloon, leaving Russell and Katina outside the undertaker's shop in the drizzling rain, silent with their own thoughts. As the late Sunday afternoon traffic of carts, wagons, mules, and pedestrians worked its way here and there with the usual clamor, neither Russell nor Katina could move.

Katina's only female friend was dead. Meg would never again peer through the door and ask about the plays, would never again offer to help with pinning laundry to the wires behind the tenement. Katina crossed her arms, bowed her head, and cried silently. At last, she spoke through parched lips. "Where are you going to get money for the burial?"

"I have a little," said Russell.

"It was her husband who beat her to death."

"Indeed? Have they other children?"

"No, the baby would have been the first."

"That's good, there will be no little ones left without a parent when the man is imprisoned."

"It is good," said Katina. "The man is a brute. I loved Mrs. Brandermill. The man is an animal, and never deserved her."

"There has to be a way," said Russell, lifting his gaze to the sky as if there might be a message etched in the clouds. Katina watched him and found herself once more attracted to this man, to his rugged face, his strong voice, his air of determined compassion for others. His canvas coat and the front of the white shirt visible beneath it were smeared with blood, but it didn't seem to offend him. "There must be a way."

"A way for what?" asked Katina.

Russell looked down then at Katina, and she was startled with the crystal clarity of his blue eyes. "A way to change circumstances. To make a difference. William, I need help."

"Help for what? To alert the authorities about Mr. Brandermill?"

"You'll do that. I mean help for a greater task."

Katina didn't have the energy to ask him what he meant. She suddenly felt dizzy. Stars swam in her vision. She couldn't pass out. She wouldn't. She'd seen worse than this in her life, and she was still standing.

"Listen," said Russell, putting his hand on Katina's shoulder. It made her feel better; it made her feel safe. She wished he would keep his hand there for a long time. "I haven't had a midday meal. Would you care to join me? Alert a constable about Mr. Brandermill. Take as long as you need. His poor wife deserves to have the truth known. Then come to Sallee's Butcher Shop on Fifth and go up the steps on the side. My apartment is at the top."

Katina stammered, "Well . . . well, I . . ."

"Have you got better plans for dinner?" asked Russell. Then he smiled a small smile, and Katina realized that he knew she had nowhere to go for a good meal. He was teasing because he could see she was as scrawny as any person in this area of Chicago, and he knew that free food was always welcome.

"I'd be happy to come," she said. "I have some bread in my flat that I can bring."

"No," said Russell. He reached out and tousled her hat, nearly knocking it off, and she was instantly chagrined. For a moment she'd forgotten she was charading as a boy, and she had imagined that he'd seen her as Katina, not William. "Bring nothing, lad. And the next time, you will cook for me."

"All right," said Katina. "I won't be long."

Although the city of Chicago was well supplied with fire-alarm boxes which citizens could use to alert the courthouse in the event of a fire, there was no such system for alerting the police department of crimes. Katina had to walk for twenty-five minutes before she found a constable. She described the beating death of Mrs. Brandermill at the hands of her husband. Although the policeman agreed to talk to Mr. Brandermill, Katina could tell he did not feel the same urgency she did.

"Thank you," he said simply. "I'll look into it."

"You will arrest him?"

"I will talk with him to see if I need to arrest him."

Katina clenched her fists. "*Need* to arrest him? Listen to me! He did it, his wife confirmed that as she lay dying, but he will surely lie."

"That is for us to determine," he said, his mustache twitching.

"Are you bribed, too?" Katina cried. "Are you going to ignore it because the criminals here have paid you to leave well enough alone?"

The policeman grabbed her arm. "Don't you speak

to me like that, boy! I'll haul you in for anything I'd like, don't think I won't. Now, get out of my way. I'll speak to Mr. Brandermill and hear his side of the story."

"Make sure you go to the undertaker's shop on Jackson Street and see Mrs. Brandermill's side of the story!" She retorted.

Her body shaking with frustration, Katina walked to Sallee's Butcher Shop. She knew this store, and had even purchased some scrap meat here. It was on the same block of Fifth Avenue as the theater, only six buildings up the street. Katina wondered if Russell had ever been in the audience. Was he even aware of the theater? Or worse, did he know the theater was there but considered drama to be trivial and a waste of time?

*Good heavens,* she scolded herself as she climbed the steps. *What difference can it make? This man can never be more than a casual acquaintance. What does it matter what he thinks of plays or theater?*

She knocked on the door and was greeted with a "Come in, if you are William. If you are a burglar, then don't come in, for I've nothing worth stealing."

Katina pushed the door open and went inside.

There were two rooms, the front room a combined kitchen and sitting area, and the second, visible through an open door, a tiny bedroom. The furniture was no better than Katina's own, scratched and mismatched. Two chairs had been pulled up to a small wooden table in the front room. There were no windows here, but the room was brightened, surprisingly, by two dark yellow roses and a cluster of purple violets in a small pottery vase. Something was at a rolling boil in a pot on the cookstove, and Russell was digging at the contents with a metal spoon.

"Hello," he said, stirring furiously. The front of his hair had curled up with the steam. "I thought I would make a soup. But I'm afraid it's out of control. Most of the water is cooked away and I've no more water in the bucket. The vegetables are sticking to the pan. This is foul!"

Katina's heart began to beat faster as she realized she was alone with Russell in his apartment. "It doesn't smell bad."

"Smell can be deceiving," said Russell.

Katina took off her coat and began to remove her hat but stopped. Not that a hat held the secret to her identity, but it helped. She'd have to show bad manners and keep it on. She hoped Russell didn't ask her about it.

"Curses," said Russell. "Look at this. A mushy disaster." He lifted the spoon. The vegetables had cooked down into something reminiscent of pig slop. "What do you think? Food fit for bachelors?"

"Of course," said Katina. "I've had worse."

Russell plopped scoopfuls of the once-soup into two bowls, handed one to Katina, and sat down across from her at the table with the other. "Oh, but you haven't tasted it yet."

Katina lifted the spoon that was on the table beside her and dipped it into the steaming mess in the bowl. Before she could lift the spoon to her lips, Russell was saying, "Lord, bless this food, such as it is, to the nourishment of our bodies and the strength of our hearts. Take Mrs. Brandermill into your arms forever. Amen."

"Amen," echoed Katina. Then she glanced up at him. He was looking at her with his intense blue eyes. He smiled, and she managed a smile back. Then he took a bite of the vegetables, grimaced, and wheezed, "Not bad."

Katina smiled, then tasted a mouthful. It was all she could do to swallow. The flavor was that of ash, tin, and scalded peas. She knew how to cook; it was one of the skills she'd learned at Willowbrook Orphan Asylum. But she couldn't admit that to Russell.

"Fond of that hat?" asked Russell around another mouthful of the food.

"Oh." Katina touched the brim and shrugged. "It's a gift from . . . my brother." *My brother?* she thought. *Now you are going to lie out loud to him? Be quiet, don't go making things up or it'll only be worse.*

"You have family in Chicago, then?" asked Russell.

"Oh, yes," Katina answered. *This is probably the truth. The Monroes on Michigan are most likely relatives.*

"I've family in the city, too," said Russell, tipping his head toward the vase with the roses and violets. "Those are from my mother's garden. My parents live across the South Branch of the river, on De Koven Street. My mother always has a beautiful flower garden, always in bloom two weeks before her neighbors. I visit my parents once a week."

"I see."

"So, are you employed, William Monroe?"

"Yes, at Anderson's Market. But also"—she slowed

her breathing so she wouldn't sound as uneasy as she did in revealing her true passion—"I'm a writer for the MacPherson Theater, on this very street. An actor also, but mainly a writer. It's what I love to do most."

"A writer?" Russell sat straight.

"Yes," said Katina. "Of plays. Someday I will create a brilliant drama that will be talked about everywhere. I will be rich and famous!"

Russell was silent for a moment, his gaze going to the far wall. *What is he thinking?*

Katina interrupted the silence. "Enough about me. How long have you lived in this place?"

"Nearly a month." Russell looked back at her and wiped his mouth on his sleeve, something Katina was sure he wouldn't have done had he known he was in a lady's company. "You say you are a writer?"

Katina nodded. "Coming here was your choice?"

"Yes. I felt drawn here, or sent, I'm not sure which. I have work to do," he finished firmly.

"What kind of work?"

Russell stirred his spoon in his vegetables. Then he said, "Do you believe things happen for a reason, William? That people are brought into situations for a purpose?"

"I'm not sure what you mean."

"You and me meeting last night, for example," Russell said. "A chance meeting, one might think, but think again. There could be destiny involved."

"You mean fate, like a gypsy's prediction?"

"No, I mean true destiny. That if we live life with

our eyes open, we will come upon things that are supposed to be there for us, things to help us continue."

Katina looked for a napkin with which to wipe her mouth, but Russell had put out none, so she used her sleeve as well. "I never thought about it."

Russell's expression shifted to one of hesitant excitement, and this made his face look like that of a little boy. "Listen," he said. "I haven't told anybody this yet, but I moved here, having quit college, because I felt called to do something about the terrible conditions of the people here."

"Who do you think you are," she asked, laughing unintentionally in disbelief, "some kind of preacher or miracle worker?"

"Between you and me, I don't know what I am."

"Do you earn a wage somewhere?"

Russell said, "Not at the moment. I've been busy trying to determine how to go about my task, getting to know the people, the establishments. Trying to convince the *Tribune* to publish an article. I've been trying alone and making little progress. Until today. When you came to the defense of Mrs. Brandermill, I saw something that impressed me. And now, I discover, you are a writer."

"What does being a writer have to do with anything?"

"My own words are clumsy. I want a story in the *Tribune* about the plight of our neighbors. There are many poor in Chicago, but many rich as well. I want the wealthy to stop for a moment and look at the poor, and see how much they could help if they only would.

I've tried to talk to reporters, with no luck. But if I had someone who could take my words and make them speak with clarity and force, then . . ."

"Wait just a moment," said Katina. Her heart skipped a beat. She had a fleeting image of Russell sitting beside her, reading her writing and marveling, of him touching her arm in appreciation. Of them spending time together, sharing meals, being close. "I have a job," she said, shaking the images from her head. "I have enough trouble taking care of myself. I might defend a friend—which clearly did no good—and I might write plays, but I'm not up to whatever your grand vision might be."

"William, you may be young, but you are feisty. And kindhearted. I need a writer, playwright or otherwise. And I need someone who will help me secure a building and create a safe haven for those like Mrs. Brandermill and Bruce Charles. If we don't help, who will?"

"You can't save the world."

"I can do what I can do."

"But you have no true sense of who I am."

"I sense you are someone good."

Katina looked at the floor. She suddenly smelled fire, and heard the crackling of flames. But it was not the burned meal nor Russell's cookstove behind her. It was an old fire, burning in her memory, mocking her in her inability to help her mother. Her sister. They were dying in a flame as she sat helpless in a tree. Doing nothing. Watching and doing nothing.

*You did nothing.*

"You've made a mistake. I can't help anybody," Katina said finally. Her words sounded flat and hard, and she didn't care.

Russell turned his palms up in resignation. "All right. I'm making presumptions. Do you forgive me?"

Katina nodded and looked back at her vegetables. They had cooled now, and a skin had formed on the top.

"Would you like to talk about baseball?" Russell asked, trying to be cheerful. "I'm fascinated with the Chicago White Stockings. I think all young men would dream of wielding a bat and watching the ball fly. And such a salary they earn, as much as $2,500 a year. Do you think you'd like to be a baseball player when you grow up?"

*Grow up?* Katina thought glumly as he went on. *I am grown up. I'm your age nearly, yet you see a child. And a boy child at that. Will I ever be able to tell you the truth?*

*And if I do, what will you think of me then?*

*And will you ever feel your pulse race when you are near me, as I feel mine race when I am near you?*

# 6

Monday morning, Russell awoke knowing that he needed to find a job. William's questions about his work and income had left him uneasy all night. He realized that it was wrong to live on the money he'd saved from not attending college, as that money would need to go to managing the safe haven once it was established. And so, as soon as the mercantile across the street opened, he spent a dollar on a wooden box full of polish, rags, and a brush, and said to himself, "I'll be a bootblack." It was an unusual job for a young man—usually children or old men polished shoes—but the work was portable, and he could do it as often as time allowed.

With the polish box beneath his arm, he stopped at the undertaker's and gave the man three dollars for Mrs. Brandermill's coffin and burial. Then he went out to find some customers in the business district. He would work all morning, then go to the *Tribune* to try again to entice a reporter to his cause.

Bruce Charles spied him from the doorway of an empty tobacco shop, jumped into the street, and grabbed the tail of Russell's coat. "Can I come?" the boy asked after Russell explained his mission. "There are pockets to pick there, and I promise I won't hit nobody with a pipe."

"I'm not going to pick pockets," Russell explained. "I'm going to make an honest penny. If you would like to learn this trade along with me, you are welcome."

Bruce grinned and said, "Yes!"

But the gentlemen with the muddy shoes and boots trodding the wide wooden sidewalks of State Street weren't easily impressed, and it was clear they thought that a young man in a wrinkled canvas coat and a young boy with no shoes at all were up to no good. As Russell stood beside the door of Mrs. Abigail Archer's Fine French Millinery, offering shines as politely as possible, the pedestrians picked up their pace in order to pass by.

After twenty minutes, Bruce smacked Russell in the arm and said, "You ain't doin' it right! Ain't you never sold nothin' before?"

"No. And neither have you."

"Let me have a go," Bruce said. As a tall man in a top hat and split-tailed coat walked by, Bruce shouted, "You there, sir, you look like a pile of walking cow dung with them messy boots! Lemme give you a polish."

Russell jerked him back by his collar.

"What's the matter?" asked Bruce "He did look dreadful, his coat all pressed and his boots covered in slop."

"Have you never heard the term, 'You can catch more flies with honey than with vinegar'? Who would stop for someone who had just insulted him?"

"I insulted him?"

"We'll have to think of another strategy."

And so they found a spot beneath a maple tree on the side of the street. Standing here, they were waist level with the pedestrians on the plank sidewalk above. Russell instructed Bruce to be quiet while Russell spoke to passing gentlemen. "A moment, sir, to shine your shoes?"

This worked. The men on the sidewalk seemed less threatened by someone not at eye level with them, and by noon Bruce and Russell had run out of polish and had made a dollar and five cents. They were coated with the mud thrown up by passing horses and carriages, but Russell was satisfied. He gave Bruce thirty cents, at which the boy grumbled that if he'd been allowed to pick a few pockets he'd have come away with more, and sent the boy off. Russell stuck the polish box beneath his arm and walked to the Tribune Building at the corner of Dearborn and Madison.

But this day was much like Saturday. Although Russell had spent a good five minutes scraping the last bit of polish from the box and onto his own shoes and raking his fingers through his hair before entering the four-story building with its arched windows and doorways, he was given no more than curious and then irritated glances by reporters and businessmen inside. He placed the polish box beneath a bench by the wall and then asked the receptionist if there was not one reporter with whom he could speak. But she turned up her nose at him, hopped from her chair, and padded down the long hall, the bustle of her skirt bouncing. A moment later she was back with two men with trim mustaches who told Russell he was a nuisance, and that he was not welcome to return.

"I only need a minute," said Russell. "This is important."

"We haven't got a minute, sir. Leave, please."

Russell turned to look each man, in turn, directly in the eye. "How do you *know* you haven't got time for me? We haven't spoken!"

"And we won't!" said one man. "You'll have the bottoms of our shoes in your back if you do not leave."

The men took his arms, but Russell jerked free, spun on his heel, and held out his shaking fist toward them. "This whole office be damned!" he said. "You and your pomposity!" He snatched the polish box from beneath the bench and stormed out the door.

Back on the sunny street, he stared up at the building, his face flushed with fury. *How dare they?* he thought. *Why won't they even listen?*

"It's not working," he said aloud as he walked back to the butcher shop, one hand deep in the pocket of his coat, the other clenched around the handle of the polish box. His unbuttoned canvas coat flapped out behind him like the wings of a giant bird. He didn't care if the people he passed heard him talking to himself and thought him soft in the head. "Why isn't it working?" His boots pounded the ground in rhythm.

"But I can't get discouraged. There are other newspapers. Yet the *Tribune* is the most widely read. It would have been the best forum." He walked on, his thoughts racing. "Maybe I'm going at this wrong. Perhaps I should find a building first, approach the owner with the money I have left as a deposit, then open the safe haven, even if I can only afford to keep it running for a week. Perhaps a reporter would then realize there was a story, and come visit, and write it up. That must be the answer. I wasn't drawn here to have this dream die."

It was when he reached the base of the steps to his flat that he remembered the MacPherson Theater. William had mentioned it. But he knew the building was not vacant; it was a theater, a business.

"But," he said to himself, "I would guess it's not used most of the time. The actors have jobs during the day, like William. And there wouldn't be a performance every night." He felt his heart leap at the possibility.

He tucked the polish box beneath the stairs, then walked down to the theater and stood staring at the old stable from the middle of the road as growling riders and wagon drivers swerved around him. The low-roofed building was about thirty feet wide along the road, extending back at least fifty feet; its shingles looked in good repair. Next door was a pawn shop. Russell rattled the door, trying to force open a crack that was big enough to see through, but the lock held tight.

"What are you doing there? This is my building."

There was a dark-haired, lanky young man beside him, shading his face and frowning.

Russell held out his hand, but the other man would not take it. "I'm Russell Cosgrove. I meant no harm. I only wanted to see inside."

"Why do you need to see inside? Has your horse gotten away from you and crawled in through the locked door, so you must go after him?"

Russell laughed, then saw it was the wrong thing to do. The man was not smiling. "No, sir. Last evening I was talking with a member of your acting troupe, and I was curious as to the layout of the building."

"Are you an actor?"

"No."

"Why, then? With whom did you speak?"

"William Monroe," said Russell. "I'm looking for a building to use during daylight hours and occasional evenings. A place that has space and is well-built. And won't require much rent."

"And William Monroe told you this place is available during the day for little rent?"

"No. But I thought there was no harm in looking."

The other man crossed his arms, one brow up, waiting for Russell to explain.

"I have plans," Russell said, hesitating, then barging ahead. "I am going to raise contributions and open a safe haven for Chicago's poorest. I need a place where folks can have a meal, find warmth in the winter and a cool drink of water in the summer, where children who run in gangs can learn to read and write and where—"

The man shook his head. "You're talking lunacy! There has never been such a thing."

"There should be."

The man stared at Russell, then looked down. But his face seemed to be softening. "Who are you, a preacher?"

"I'm a bootblack, looking to help my neighbors."

"But this place is a theater."

"I know. Could I take a look inside?"

"I'm busy today. I'm picking up a fresh supply of nails for fences we are repairing at Tichnor's varnish shop. I was on my way to the hardware when I saw you."

"A quick look inside. Please?"

"You say you know William?"

"We shared a meal last night. May I look?"

The man took a deep, agitated breath. "All right. But only for a moment." He unlocked the door. It swung wide.

It was cool and dark inside, and the shadows Russell first took for sleeping bodies along the floor were actually rows of benches facing the back of the wide room. The smell was one of old hay, dirt, and kerosene. As his eyes adjusted, he could see the stage at the other end of the room and several lanterns on hooks along the walls beside small, latched windows. It was indeed a theater. And it was indeed a good-sized room, a place that could be a temporary safe haven until someone with wealth was willing to help purchase another, larger place.

"Do you see, Mr. Cosgrove?" asked the man. "I don't believe this would fit your needs."

Russell walked toward the stage, trying to imagine how many people could eat here, where a table might be set for tutoring. He pulled the curtain aside along the rope tie, and stepped onto the stage.

The next instant he heard a scream that froze his blood and stopped him in his tracks.

# 7

She hadn't meant to scream.

*They know I'm here now! God help me!*

She put her hand over her mouth, knowing it was futile but not knowing anything else to do. She had already screamed.

*They are going to find me!*

One man shouted, "Who was that?"

The voice sounded familiar. She took a breath and held it. On the heels of the first shout came, "Hello, who is in there?"

Katina, her face tucked inside the collar of her coat and sitting back in the far corner of the old tack stall, slowly pulled the collar down far enough to see out. There were two figures outside the stall, staring in. She knew they could see her, and she had no defense. Even her safety stick was somewhere on Quincy Street, dropped and lost when she had come to Mrs. Brandermill's defense.

There was a moment of silence, with only the sound of fluttering swallow wings in the rafters.

And then the first man's voice again. "Hello?"

"Adam?" said Katina softly.

"William?"

"Adam, it's me. If you have a gun, for heaven's sake don't shoot."

"William?" said the other man. Katina knew this voice, too. She tucked her face back inside her coat, thinking, *I am safe, thank the Lord. But why is it him? Why did he have to find me like this?*

The second voice belonged to Russell Cosgrove.

"What on God's green earth are you doing here?" asked Adam. A hand touched her shoulder, and she pulled her face out of her collar again. Adam and Russell were kneeling, looking at her as if she'd grown a second nose. Adam was squinting with his bad eyes. "Are you hurt?" he asked.

"No," said Katina. "Not yet."

"Not yet?" asked Russell.

Katina sighed painfully and said, "I should have left it alone. I shouldn't have opened my big mouth. I should have said nothing to the constable. I'm in deep trouble." She got up slowly, wriggling her toes inside her shoe to rid them of a tingling sensation. She nodded at the brocade satchel on the floor beside her.

"Everything I own," she said, "is in there. And I've no place to live."

"Did your building burn down?" asked Adam.

"No, but it might as well have." She looked Russell

directly in his eyes, and saw a concern there that almost made her cry. Almost. She would not cry in front of this man. "Mr. Brandermill was questioned by the authorities at my request, as you know. They described to him the person who alerted them. They described *me* to him. Of course, John Brandermill would be one of those who, like many other criminals in our fair neighborhood, bribe police with their gambling income to leave them alone. The man's still in the tenement, still free, and watching for me to come back so he can . . ." Katina couldn't say more. She couldn't imagine what might come after that. All she knew was that she had to hide.

Russell put his arm around her shoulder. He smelled good—of cheap soap and tenderness. "William, I'm so sorry. This is dreadful!"

Adam said, "I don't understand."

The three went to the front of the theater and sat on a bench. Katina related the story of Meg Brandermill's death. Both men agreed that it was dangerous for William now, not only because Mr. Brandermill was a violent man, but because none of them knew who his cohorts were, and how could she avoid them if she didn't even know them?

"Are you certain he knows it was you who told?"

"When I returned to the boardinghouse, I saw him looking out his window at me. I could tell by his expression that something foul was brewing in his mind."

"Then you need a place to hide," said Adam.

Katina groaned, exasperated. "Why do you think I

sneaked in here, genius? Because I prefer hard floors with scratchy straw crumbs to a bed?"

"William," said Adam, "for all your good intentions, why did you have to say anything? Mrs. Brandermill died, and nothing, not even the arrest of her husband, will bring her back. Now my theater must be shut down until he is arrested so you can be out of sight?"

"I have a better idea," said Russell. "William, come stay with me."

Katina looked at Russell sharply. "What?"

"I have space, two chairs, an extra blanket, and we can sleep head to toe if you don't mind my socks in your face. And you know what a fine cook I am."

"Oh, well, no," stammered Katina. *There is no way I could agree to share an apartment with a man!*

"And why not?" asked Adam.

"I . . ." began Katina, but she couldn't think of a plausible reason to refuse Russell's offer. She did need a place to stay, and a friend was offering it to her. But how could she live in a tiny, two-room apartment with this man and not have him discover her true identity? How could she live so close to this strong, kind, and handsome man and not find herself, well . . .

*Falling in love*, she thought. *No! It would be better just to continue to hide here in this old stable until Mr. Brandermill is dealt with.*

And so she said, "Russell, it is generous of you, but I can't afford to pay and so I can't afford to stay with you. Thank you, but I'm—"

"Don't be ridiculous," said Russell. "I wouldn't expect you to pay me in money. But I do have an idea, one that will benefit us both."

"What is that?" she asked hesitantly.

"In lieu of cash, you can write for me. You told me yourself you are a writer."

"He is a fine writer," said Adam.

"Write for me, William. I have a desk, ink, paper. My notes are in desperate need of reshaping. You can share my meals, the heat from my stove, until it is safe again for you to come out. All right?"

"I write only plays!"

"A writer can write anything, play or essay. Do you agree?"

"Of course he does," said Adam. He looked at Katina. "You do agree, don't you?"

"Agreed," Katina heard herself say.

Adam patted Katina's head, then hopped up. "I must be gone with my nails. Where do you live, sir? I shall come by later to check on our young friend."

"My flat is at the end of this block above Sallee's butcher shop. Just listen and you'll hear the owners shouting. It's hard to miss."

"Done, then," said Adam. He hurried to the door, but paused there and called over his shoulder, "William, how did you get into the theater?"

Katina pointed at a loose shutter.

Adam said, "And I thought the place was secure! Blast it all!" And then he was gone.

Katina knew she was shaking—her trembling rattled her to her teeth—but she bit the inside of her cheek to control it. *Writing as payment? Katina, be calm now. This is certainly manageable. Room and board in exchange for an essay or two?* It was more than fair.

*And yet . . . !*

Russell had gone back to the stall and now stood before Katina, holding her satchel and smiling his startlingly beautiful smile. "Let's get you settled in," he said. "This will work out well! I do believe this was meant to be. Come, William, you look as if you've swallowed something foul!"

Katina pulled her hat down low over her eyes, shrugged the collar of her coat back up to obscure her chin, and followed Russell down the street to the butcher shop. With only her eyes visible, she observed those who passed them on the street. Mothers, holding babies in tightly wrapped cloaks, headed for market. Dirty children laughed and chased each other with sticks. A young woman in her plain skirt and shawl, her own age, stood with her beau and mooned over him with starstruck eyes.

None of them seemed to be looking for her. She knew she would be safe, tucked away in Russell's apartment. *But it is all so . . . intimate, much too intimate. Sharing his table, his washbowl, his blankets.* She muffled a cough brought on by the grit rising from the road.

It was dark inside the apartment, and the air still hinted of the burned meal they'd shared the previous evening. Russell dropped the satchel on the table, went into the tiny bedroom, and pushed the curtains aside. Dim light filled the apartment.

He came back into the front and said, "My journals are on the desk by the bed. You can sort through them to see if you can make sense of the contents while I'm gone. There are pages and pages, but something a writer can hopefully put into a form that is publishable. And make yourself at home. I've a few potatoes in that bin, some cornbread, jam, some boiled eggs, and water in the bucket." He raised one eyebrow, and Katina knew he was trying hard to ease her worries. She wondered how it would feel to have him hold her close, to touch her face and caress her back. How safe that would feel. How wonderful.

*Stop thinking like that!*

Katina said, "Thank you. I appreciate all of this."

"I have things to do this afternoon," Russell continued. "I've got a potential contributor to visit, the proprietor of the Stick Saloon."

"You don't mean Madame Jocelyn."

"Do you know the woman?"

"I know of her."

"Do you think she'd be willing to make a donation?"

"Hah! You'll only know if you ask."

Russell ran his fingers through his hair. He glanced at Katina with earnest uncertainty. "Do I look all right?"

"You look quite handsome," said Katina, then quickly amended, "I mean you look good, presentable." *Oh, watch your words, Katina!*

"Good." He opened the door, then said, "I apologize if I seemed to take your concerns lightly, William.

You are probably more frightened now than at any time in your life."

"Actually, I have been more frightened, believe it or not," said Katina, giving him a tough-boy look.

"I know you feel coerced into helping me, but I appreciate it just the same."

"I'm happy to help."

And then he was gone, the door closing behind him, and she heard his heavy footsteps pounding down to the street. From below, Katina could hear a man and woman yelling at each other, something about maggots in a delivery of pig's feet.

She sat at the table, looked at the bread on the plate beneath the linen, then let the linen fall back. She had no appetite. A mouse raced across the floor and she watched it go.

"Happy to help? How can I be happy to help?" she said to herself. "I should be at Anderson's Market. Mr. Anderson is surely angry, wondering what happened to his errand boy. I shall lose that job, and when I do return he will withhold my last week's earnings as punishment." She slammed her elbows on the tabletop. "Russell Cosgrove, do you see the result of trying to do good for others? Do you see this refugee, hiding in your home, now without any income? Isn't it best to be concerned about your own welfare? Isn't that enough?"

The shouting downstairs stopped. A customer must have come into the shop.

"Fine," said Katina, looking through the door at the small desk in the corner. "I will write your articles,

Russell, and when Mr. Brandermill is in jail, I will leave you to your dreams of a safe haven. My debt will be paid."

Katina's gaze found the bright yellow roses and violets in the vase. And she wondered for a brief moment if beautiful things could really exist in a terrible place, and if a dream of hope could bloom in a world of despair.

# 8

⨒

## Police Captain's Barn, Outbuildings Consumed

South Side Police Captain Michael Logan returned to his home on Griswold Street after work Wednesday night to find his barn and several outbuildings burning to the ground and his home scorched. The cause appears to have been several boys, including Logan's own son, Michael, Jr., smoking cigars in the outhouse. Also damaged were the fruit trees in the yard, an animal pen in the neighboring yard of Mr. and Mrs. Francis LaVin, and a thirty-five-foot stretch of wooden sidewalk along the road.

Firemen responded quickly with their steam engine, the "Little Colonel." The flames were extinguished within the hour thanks to the quick action of the men, though Captain Logan said that for a mo-

⨒

ment he had a vision of the burning sidewalk not going out and the fire racing up the street like a bandit with a bag full of gold.

"I've seen fires in our city before," Logan laughed nervously, "but only in the instant when my own home was ablaze and the walk in front of my yard was alight, did I truly realize how much wood there is in the city! Why, we are just a forest of dead trees, stacked up and nailed down and piled high!"

Captain Logan spoke correctly that Chicago is a city made of wood. At this date, the council reports that we have over 55 miles of pine block streets and 600 miles of wooden sidewalks, not to mention the majority of buildings are constructed of wood, also. But the citizens of Chicago can rest easy, knowing that in spite of inevitable fires, our water system, our fire alarms, and our brave firemen with their hoses and wagons can be trusted to keep even the worst blazes at bay.

—George Rainey, *Chicago Tribune*,
June 6, 1871

Madame Jocelyn was not as old as Methuselah, but she seemed to come close. She had white hair, which she covered with a bright orange hat held in place by a jeweled stickpin. Her wrinkled mouth and cheeks were boldly red, and she wore a corset so tight that Russell was amazed she could draw a breath.

He sat across a table from her in the Stick Saloon,

sipping a cup of hot tea. Regular customers sat at other tables and at the long wooden bar, trying to sing along to the tune a girl was banging out on the piano. Alice Montague and Becky Alaimo were serving drinks. Smoke from pipes clung to the sooty ceiling like cobwebs.

"I don't understand what you are asking, Mr. Cosgrove," the woman said, pursing her red, prunish lips and glaring. "You want to do *what?*"

"Open a place to serve those who live here. It's a charitable gesture, and I thought you might be willing to make a donation."

"Have other saloon owners been approached?"

"Yes."

"And?"

"They've offered nothing."

"I thought not." She lifted her glass and took a long gulp. Russell could tell her tea was laced with something much stronger. "There will always be the poor, Mr. Cosgrove. There is nothing we can do about it."

"So Pastor Botkins says. I don't believe it."

"Oh?" One black-lined brow went up. "You don't?" She drained the remainder of her drink, belched, and called, "Becky! More for me! Mr. Cosgrove, more whiskey?"

"No, thank you, I've having *tea.*"

"Yes, *tea.* Are you sure?"

"I'm sure."

Russell thought he should leave. He'd been here half an hour, and she was no more willing than the other saloon owners to share her wealth. She might not be throwing him to the street or knifing him, but she was toying with him, and that was just as bad. *One last try and then I'll go.* "I believe I've found a building," he said. "But I need a big table or two, and chairs."

"Indeed," Madame Jocelyn snorted. "You are too handsome a man to be worried about anything but ladies."

Russell ignored this. "I need a cookstove and pots and utensils. I also need books, paper, pens and ink, blankets, clothes—cast-off but in decent condition . . ."

Madame Jocelyn linked her fingers behind her head. There was a hole in the dress beneath her arm. "You sound like a missionary on his way to save a savage country! Glory, hallelujah!"

"That is exactly what I am trying to do. But the savage country is outside those doors, not in some faraway jungle."

Madame Jocelyn gave Russell a conspiratorial look. "Will it get me into heaven, helping you?"

"That is not something any person can answer." *This was a waste of my time and hers*, Russell thought. He stood up and bowed. "Thank you for your time, ma'am."

Alice Montague, dressed in a bright green dress and lopsided lace cap, came to the table with a decanter and poured Madame Jocelyn a nearly full glass. She waited until the old woman said, "And just what do you want?"

"I wondered if you'd heard about the dead woman," Alice replied, glancing at Russell.

"What dead woman?"

"Mrs. Brandermill," said Alice. "Beaten to death yesterday by her husband. Don't you know her husband, Madame Jocelyn? I've heard you talk about him."

"Brandermill? John Brandermill!" said Madame Jocelyn. "In a world of lyin', cheatin' men, he's one of the worst. He'd kill his grandfather for a chew of tobacco!"

"I thought you should know that Mr. Cosgrove here tried to save his poor wife," said Alice. "Took her to St. Andrew's as she was dyin', to find help for her. Yelled at the reverend when the man wouldn't do anything."

"You tried to save John Brandermill's wife?" asked Madame Jocelyn, looking at Russell with one penciled-in eyebrow raised.

"Well, yes," said Russell.

"John Brandermill beat his wife and you tried to help her, out in front of God and everybody?"

"Oh, yes, indeed," said Alice.

"Most folks would have let her alone, knowing it was John Brandermill's wife, his handiwork. Good for you."

"Thank you."

Madame Jocelyn waved her hand. "Write out what you need. Any enemy of John Brandermill's is a friend of mine."

Alice grinned broadly. Russell mouthed, "Thank you!"

Outside in the fresh air, Russell shook his head and smiled. "I'm going to get the supplies," he said in wonder. He looked back at the Stick Saloon and saw Alice peeking out of an upstairs window. She waved. He waved back. Then he set off down the street toward his apartment. *The next thing*, he thought, *is to secure a place*. It wouldn't do to have a wagon dump chairs and pans in the road because he wasn't ready.

The air had grown humid with the onset of evening. It smelled like rain again. From open windows and sagging doorways, mothers called for children to come in for dinner. Men lit cigars on the side of the street, while others retreated to the bright allure of the dance halls and gambling houses. Russell pulled his hands up into his sleeves as he hurried home to tell William his news. During the past weeks, this kind of weather had beaten him down. He had even begun to feel less than certain about his reasons for coming to this slum.

But tonight was different. Tonight there was a friend waiting at home. For the first time in a month he didn't feel lonely. He felt, at that moment, that he could accomplish anything.

Russell went into the Sallees' shop before going upstairs. Lieutenant Sallee was behind the meat counter, wiping his face on his bloody apron. The place was a mixture of sights and scents. Sausages, bacon, and smoked fish were strung from the ceiling. In the glass counter were chickens, unrecognizable chunks of fatty meats, and tripe. Some was fresh, and some spoiled; the combination gave off a tart, salty smell that swam in Russell's head.

"Hello," said Russell. Lieutenant dropped the apron and looked up as if he knew something was wrong.

"Is something the matter with the apartment?"

"Not at all. I want to buy some meat," said Russell. "That chicken there. I'm celebrating tonight."

"Celebrating? You can't celebrate in my building!"

Russell laughed. "How much for the chicken?"

The man snorted like a bull, then pulled out the tray on which several plucked chickens sat. "Which one?"

Russell pointed. The butcher took out the meat and put it on the scale, saying, "You pay by weight, you know."

"I know."

"That's a four-pound chicken."

"Would you weigh it again, sir," said Russell as pleasantly as he could. "Without pushing down with your hand?"

Lieutenant snarled, moved his hand from the top of the chicken, and read the scale again. "Three pounds," he said. "And that was an accident, my hand being there!"

Russell paid for the chicken and carried it upstairs. The lantern was not lit; the apartment was pitch-black. He put the bird on the table and glanced around, squinting. "William?"

There was a faint answer from the back room. "Here."

"What are you doing in the dark?"

"What do you think? I'm hiding. I heard someone on the steps and I wasn't sure it was you."

Russell struck a match from the shelf over the stove, sending a brief whiff of phosphorus, then a glow. He touched the flame to the wick in the lantern.

There was a shuffling sound, and William appeared

in the bedroom doorway. He still wore his coat and hat.

"You have been there all afternoon?"

"No, only since it got dark."

Russell pointed to the bird on the table. "I bought a chicken to celebrate the successful day. Madame Jocelyn has offered to donate some items for the safe haven. So I thought, instead of my usual fare of burned soup, we would have a feast tonight."

"Celebrate?" said William without smiling. "Why not? I'm stuck here, unable to go outside for a breath of fresh air until John Brandermill has forgotten me. Dandy!"

Russell sighed as he took off his coat. "What else can we do?" he asked. "If you can think of something else, tell me and I'll be glad to assist. Or leave, if that would make you happy. I don't want you beaten up or killed, but I'm not your jailer."

William looked at the floor. He seemed so vulnerable, with his hands crammed into the pockets of his trousers. Russell had the urge to go comfort the boy, but he didn't think such a gesture would be welcome.

"Would you help me cook?" Russell asked finally.

"I better," said William. He looked up at last and tried to smile. "You tried to make me sick with that dreadful soup of yours. Who knows how much damage you could do with a whole chicken!"

# 9

Adam MacPherson stopped by at eight o'clock, ate a piece of the boiled chicken, and then agreed that, for two dollars and a free boot polish a week, Russell could use the theater. He made Russell promise to limit the number of people he would allow inside at once, fearing mobs would split the place down the sides.

"I'll be checking on you," Adam said. "You offer free food and there is going to be mayhem."

"I'll be sure the place is cared for," said Russell. "It will be hard, but I have to start somewhere."

Adam gave Russell an extra key to the theater, bid the two a good evening, and left.

Russell waved his fork at the ceiling and cheered, "The plan is succeeding! I knew it would. I believe some things are meant to be, and this is one of them. Your friend Adam is a fine fellow. I won't take his trust lightly."

"I hope it works out for you," Katina said. It was hard to listen to Russell's plans. Her thoughts raced back and forth like a dog in a cage, going over and over the same ground. *I've lost my job at Anderson's. I have no home to call my own. John Brandermill is looking for me in order to hurt me, maybe kill me!*

"For us," said Russell. Then he paused and gave Katina a long look. "I hope it is for us, not just me. You are trapped here for a while, true. And I know you've agreed to help me by writing only out of necessity. But I hope it becomes meaningful to you, too. When you see the faces on the children, William, the old people . . ."

"Don't call me that."

"Don't call you what?"

*I'm Katina!* "Nothing, I don't know, I'm tired," she answered. *Nobody knows the true me! The Monroe family on Michigan Avenue think I'm an insane woman with designs on their family fortune. Everybody thinks I'm a boy! What kind of life is this?*

"We're both tired. It's time for bed," said Russell.

Katina got up from the table, washed the dishes in a pan of hot water, used his brittle straw broom to sweep the floor, then found a rag and began to wipe the table.

"Are you expecting President Grant?" asked Russell from the bedroom.

"No," said Katina.

"Enough, then! I can't bear all this cleanliness."

Katina put the rag on the shelf. Clearly it was time to sleep. *How am I going to manage that?*

Russell opened the bedroom window a crack. A cool

breeze poured through and into the front room, countering the steamy air in the apartment. He called, "I don't have a wardrobe for your clothes, but I've got a trunk. You can put your clothes in there."

"I don't have many clothes," said Katina.

"Maybe not, but they won't do, all rolled up in your satchel." *The satchel!* Katina instantly realized what was going to happen. She ran to the bedroom door and saw Russell unbuckling the satchel on the bed. "I'll put your clothes in the trunk with mine. They won't grow sour in there."

"No!" Katina dashed to the bedside and grabbed the satchel. "I don't want my clothes in the trunk."

Russell's eyes widened. "There aren't any mice in there."

"I don't care. I—I'll keep my things in here if it's all the same to you."

Russell shrugged. "That's fine with me. Although it makes little sense."

*It makes a great deal of sense to me!* Katina thought. *My skirt is in there, and my blouse, and my writings!*

Russell lit the bedroom lantern, sat down on the bed, and took off his shoes. Katina turned to look out the window. She could see the tainted haze of light that settled over the city at night. Light from candles in tenement windows. Light from lanterns in passing wagons or in the hands of nighttime pedestrians. Light from the bows of the ships that rode the river to the west and north. Light from the frequent fires that plagued the city, burning down a shack here, a warehouse there, before the fire engines could arrive to put them out. The combined light rose above the city's buildings in a vague canopy, mingling with the mist from the lake and blurring the stars and moon.

*God,* she thought. *Help me know what to do. I need something good for once in my life. I'm tired of fears and worry.*

"Are you coming to bed?" asked Russell.

She turned around. Russell was sitting on the bed, his chest bare and his shirt folded neatly beside him. He was leaning forward, his arms resting on his thighs, his fingers linked. His body was beautiful in the lantern light, with lines of firm muscles just beneath the skin of his chest and abdomen. She drew in a sharp breath, hoping he could not see her surprise or the sudden longing that had caused her heart to pick up its beat. Then she saw that his right arm was bandaged, and that blood had seeped through the cloth.

"What happened to your arm?" she asked.

"Just a scuffle over at Bunch's Bar."

"Does it hurt?"

He shrugged.

Katina walked to the bed. "May I see it, to make sure it's healing properly?"

"And how would you know that, Master Monroe?" Russell gave a dubious smile, a strand of his dark brown hair falling into his eyes. Katina wished she could say, *Because the girls at Willowbrook were taught how to care for injuries.* But she only said, "Curiosity."

Russell slowly unwrapped the bandage, barely hiding his grimace as he did so. Katina said, "It's full of pus. Have you changed the bandage since you wrapped it?"

"No."

"Let me try something," Katina said. She went into the front room, got a clean rag, and dipped it in the water bucket, then came back to the bed and, with Russell tightening his fists, began to wipe out the wound.

"Miss Innis had an unusual idea about the care of wounds," said Katina, feeling a need to talk to keep her mind off what she was doing. "She believed it was better to air out a cut and to wash it often. She believed evil spirits came into a cut if it wasn't kept clean. Strange! She was quite the character."

"Who is Miss Innis?" asked Russell.

Katina's hands froze over the wound. Was there anything she could say to this man that wouldn't give her away? "Oh, an old friend, from long ago."

"Interesting," he said. Katina looked at Russell. His head was tilted to one side, his gaze questioning. "And you, William, are a very interesting person. There is something strange about you, but I can't determine quite what it is."

Katina went back to work. Her throat felt tight, and she knew her face was flushed. She was touching him, holding his strong arm with its warm skin and surprisingly soft hair. Russell held still, breathing through his teeth, even as she dug deep into the blood-red wound to clean it out. It took two strips of clean rag to bandage it back up when she had finished. She tied the ends securely but not too tight. Then she took the dirty rag out to the front room and rinsed it in the bucket.

"I'll toss out the water in the morning," said Russell.

"All right." She turned the wick down in the front-room lantern, extinguishing the light. In the darkness, her heartbeats were all the louder in her temples, and it was all she could do to keep her breathing in check. She wanted to go back in his room and touch him again. She wanted to hold that arm, to put her head on that bare shoulder, and to feel his own arms draw in around her.

"I've given you my pillow," came the voice from the darkness in the other room. "And the blanket is plenty large. I promise not to kick you."

Katina stood still beside the stove.

"William? Have you run off?"

"I'll sleep out here on the floor," she said at last.

"You must be teasing."

"No. I'll be fine. I can use my coat as a blanket."

"Why?"

She didn't know what to say. She went to the corner, curled up on the bare wood floor, and tried to snuggle down inside her jacket. She removed her hat and balled it up into a worthless pillow. He would never touch her as she'd imagined. She had to know that, to accept that. Tears sprang to her eyes and she brushed them away.

"Why, William?"

She didn't answer. It was best to let him think she'd already fallen asleep.

Minutes later, there were footsteps beside her, a hand touching the top of her head, and the scent of Russell's cheap soap. He whispered, "You are a funny fellow, William Monroe. I hope someday to know you better." And then a blanket was being draped over her, there was one last pat on her head, and he was gone.

She lay in the dark with his blanket, feeling the tingle from his touch long into the night.

# 10

"I've named him Stump," said Russell as he put the little black puppy down on the floor, and the puppy immediately licked Katina's hand and wagged its wrapped, nearly nonexistent tail. "I rescued him from two teenaged boys outside the theater. They'd cut off his tail. I thought he'd fare better with us."

Katina picked up the dog and buried her face in his smelly, warm fur. "How dreadful, the poor animal!"

"He can be company for you in your captivity," said Russell. He sat on the table beside the journal papers Katina had been sorting through all morning. She had read them all, but had only come up with a title, "A Case for Charity in Chicago." She'd written several sentences, but had scratched them all out.

"I wish you could see everything Madame Jocelyn has sent! As I was cleaning out the brush at the side of the building, a grumpy old gentleman came up in a wagon full of goods and told me Madame Jocelyn said he had to drive these over or she'd never let him step foot in the Stick again."

Russell hopped off the table and began pacing back and forth. "There's a large oval table, terribly marred but with legs sturdy enough to hold a bear. There's an iron stove, some cast-off clothes from her working girls. Frilly, lacy things with rips from stem to stern, but I think if we could find a lady good with a needle, we could transform them into suitable dresses."

"I see," said Katina. The daylight and Russell's enthusiasm had lifted her spirits a bit, and she told herself she should be content now, at this moment, to be safe and cared for. To think about anything more would just make her miserable.

"Several pairs of shoes, lantern oil, a frying pan, and several cooking pots. Five wool blankets with barely a hole. Other things I can't remember. Some utensils. I've decided to call the safe haven Homeplace. Does that sound welcoming?"

Katina nodded and put the wiggling Stump on the floor. The puppy went to the water bucket and began to drink. "What now?"

"I've locked the theater. The place won't be ready until we've decided our next step. I haven't gotten any food at all yet, so we can't serve meals. We don't have paper or pens or books yet, so we can't teach lessons."

*He's still saying "we,"* Katina thought. She found herself smiling.

Russell stopped pacing at her smile, and his matched hers. "This is going to work, don't you think?"

"It will. There are few people with your determination. You amaze me."

"I do?" He came over to stand beside her and look at the papers she had spread on the table. His hair had been combed earlier, but the wind had tossed it, and a few strands hung over one brow, giving him a carefree appearance. His eyes sparkled with cheerful purpose. "How is the writing going?"

"Actually, it's not, yet," said Katina. "I've told you I write plays. The audience for this is educated, academic. It will be a challenge, but I'll try my best."

Russell put his arm around her shoulder. "I do wish you could come down to Homeplace to see what is developing. I wish there was some way, a trick we could use, a disguise to get you outside safely."

"A disguise is just what I need." She nearly laughed with the irony, but bit her tongue.

"Well," Russell said, moving away and picking up his polish box from the floor by the door, "I have to get on." As he pulled the front door open, a strong wind rushed in and blew Katina's papers across the tabletop until she dove on them. "I have to canvass the area and determine who we should first invite to Homeplace, the most needy. I need to polish a few shoes to buy some dry goods. And I plan on going by your old tenement house to see if Brandermill is still a free man. I'll be back in time for dinner."

Katina watched the door close, looked at the scattered papers, then looked into the bedroom. A disguise, he had said. How could someone already disguised disguise himself—herself—and not be recognized?

Her pulse picked up.

"No, I can't," she told the puppy, who had found a mouse under the stove and was digging for it. "If I do, I can never go back to being William again. But why would that be so terrible?"

*You can't be sure of what will happen if you change. You are safer as a boy. You have friends.*

"But I don't have myself."

Stump barked at the stove, then curled up in the corner.

"I am Katina Monroe," Katina said. It sounded frightening, but she got up anyway. She took her satchel from the corner, opened it, and took out the blouse and skirt. Slowly she stepped out of her trousers and shirt and walked naked to the back room where Russell had a small looking glass on his desk. She held it up and stared at herself for a long time. This was who she was, not William the boy, but Katina the woman. And she was surprised to see her mother's beautiful eyes gazing back at her.

"In taking on a new disguise," she said to the woman in the mirror, "I will lose my disguise."

The afternoon was excruciatingly long. Wearing her skirt, blouse, and scarf, she sat at the front-room table and made herself concentrate on the article. *If only I could make this into a play*, she thought, *I could do this*. A play about a child in Conley's Patch and his dog, and the rich man who came to his aid and saved his life. She could write something like that.

The late June afternoon grew cloudy, so she lit the

lantern, determined to ignore the noises from the street below, and tried to write. Stump woke, chewed at the bandage on his tail, then went back to sleep.

There were footsteps on the stairs. Katina dropped the pen and ran into the bedroom. She stood behind the door, waiting, listening. Was it dinnertime? How long had she pondered over the essay? She held her breath.

*What will he think?*

The door unlocked with a rattle and then swung open. Katina watched through the crack between the bedroom door and the frame, feeling suddenly afraid.

*What if he is angry at the lie?*

"William?" called Russell. "Hey, Stump, where is he?" Russell glanced around, taking off his coat and dropping it on a chair. "You must be here, the lantern is burning." He shook his head. "I could guess that you are playing a game at hiding from me, but how much of a game is it when there are so few places to hide? Under the bed or behind the door."

Katina cleared her throat silently and stepped into the doorway.

Russell, who had been holding the dog, put him down slowly. He stared at her, emotions flowing across his face like waves on the lake. He said, "William, what an amazing disguise. It's incredible, it's just—" He stopped, then took a step forward. Katina did the same. The skin on her arms danced in trepidation and hope.

"Russell," she said softly.

Russell tilted his head in wonder. "It *is* a disguise, isn't it?" he asked.

Slowly Katina shook her head.

"You . . . you are William, are you not?"

"For a time I was," said Katina. "For more than a year now, after I came here from Georgia. But I've been acting. I had to, for reasons of safety, and then privacy. But now I am in need of a disguise, so I can be myself again."

"Who are you?"

"My name is Katina. Katina Monroe."

Russell spun around, and stared at the front wall. Katina could see his shoulders moving up and down with his controlled breathing.

"Do you think I'm ugly?" she asked finally.

Russell said, "I don't know what I think."

"This must be quite a shock." *Oh, God, don't let him hate me!* "I am eighteen," she continued, her voice more steady than she could have hoped. "My father died as a Confederate soldier, and my mother and sister were burned alive by Northern renegades. I've lived half my life in a home for orphans, then I came to Chicago when I found reason to believe I had relatives living here."

His back still turned, Russell said, "But why disguise yourself as a boy?"

"You seem to understand the lengths people must often go to in order to survive. I came to Chicago after my family was slaughtered. Yet my relatives here would have nothing to do with me, declaring I was a lying opportunist, although I hope still to win them over. But I had to make a choice. Boys on their own fare better than girls. Would you have had me work like Alice or Becky?"

Russell said nothing.

"It doesn't matter if you approve. I did what I had to do." As she spoke the words, she could feel her heart twisting inside out. It shouldn't matter what he thought, but it did. It mattered very much.

"I see," said Russell.

"I suppose it's done, then." Katina came into the front room, took her satchel from the chair, scratched Stump's ear, and said, "I've got your essay begun, though barely. Use it if you'd like, or start again. I'll be safe now. John Brandermill is not looking for a woman."

She was moving for the door when his hand grabbed her wrist. She turned to face the tall man, and she could see his face had softened, so much that she wondered if he might have tears in his eyes.

"Katina," he said.

"What?"

"I believe things happen for a reason. Destiny, good and bad things, coming together to teach us and move us in the right direction. You didn't come here by mistake."

"No?"

He shook his head. "And I'd still like you to help, if you are willing."

"I am willing to try."

He let go of her wrist, took a long, deep breath, then shook his head and smiled. "I always thought there was something different about you. I just didn't know what."

And then, to Katina's surprise, he reached out and

stroked her face and touched her hair, not as an adult would touch a child, but in a new way. A way that made her breath catch and the flesh of her body stand at attention, waiting, hopeful.

He moved his hands to her shoulders, and his face softened, and she thought, *Yes, he's going to kiss me!*

But then he stepped back as if coming out of a trance and said, "You realize you can't stay here now, that's for certain."

"No," said Katina. Her words were shaky. "But I'll find somewhere."

"I know a place that is noisy, but there are two young ladies there who I believe would give you a bed if we ask."

"The Stick?"

Russell nodded. "But please make it clear that you are only looking for a place to sleep, not a job!"

Katina said, "Of course not." She knew he was right, although at the Stick she would no longer see him every day. *It is all right*, she told herself. *He knows the truth. And he doesn't hate me.*

"Madame Jocelyn is tough," Russell said. "So if I ask I'm sure she'll keep you safe from rowdy patrons. Her customers are afraid of her, and she likes me."

Katina chuckled. "I hope they aren't too shocked to see me as me."

"I do, too. And, Katina?"

"Yes?"

"You aren't ugly. Quite the contrary."

Outside, the evening air was heavy with summer mist. Rain was on its way again. As Russell locked the door behind them, Katina wrapped her arms around herself and felt the humid air tickling her ankles. *Ah, boy's clothes are so much more comfortable.*

And then an arm took hers, and the touch was tender and warmer than sunshine, and Katina thought, *This may work out for the best after all. Things will never be the same, but I don't feel as afraid as I thought I would. Perhaps this is destiny. God bless destiny.*

# 11

Late July had settled on Chicago with an intensity that dried up all traces of mud and good humor, sent shadows fleeing into corners, and sucked the energy from every living creature. Horses hung their heads as if only their harnesses kept them standing, pigeons hid under eaves, and on the streets of the business district ladies tried their best, in vain, not to perspire. Rain was nowhere to be found.

Katina sat at the large table inside the MacPherson Theater with Bruce Charles, a nine-year-old girl named Caroline, and a pair of soot-covered twelve-year-old twins, Gregory and Gerrard Cruikshank. All the small windows were propped open to let in whatever tiny breeze might happen along, but the children were fidgety in the heat, and Katina had to struggle to keep her attention focused as well as theirs.

*I'm not a teacher*, she thought. *I'm no good at this.*

"Try again, Bruce," she said, pointing to a word in a book of poetry. "You know this."

Bruce shrugged. "Why do I want to read poetry? What good will it do me?"

"It doesn't matter what we read for practice," said Katina. "The point is to learn to read, whether a history book or a bill of sale. That way you will not be taken advantage of and you will earn respect. Try again."

Bruce rolled his eyes, making the other children giggle, and looked at the book. "Roses," he read in a halting voice.

> *"Roses grow upon the wall,*
> *Borne on stems both green and tall;*
> *Their blooms are lovely, red and sweet,*
> *Yet their thorns a bane to meet."*

"Fine," said Katina.

"We've read and done numbers for hours and hours today!" said Gregory. "It's too hot. Can we stop?"

Katina shut the book, wiped her hand across her sweaty forehead, and said, "All right. I'll see you tomorrow, same time. And no pocket-picking!"

The four children skittered out of the theater to the dusty street.

"You're good with them kids," said Becky Alaimo. She was sitting on one of the benches, snapping beans for the midday meal and dropping them into a bowl at her feet. Alice was next to her, shelling peas. Stump sat by the bowl, watching the peas fall in.

Katina pushed her sleeves up to her elbows, trying to cool off. She wore a dress that Alice had given her, one she'd had to modify so it was not quite so daring. She continued to wear a scarf around her hair, which had grown out an inch and was now puffy and hard to manage. "But I'm not, really," she said. "The safe haven's been open since the end of June. And it's nearly August. We serve a meal to thirty people a day, but turn twice as many away. We want to teach children, but I am the only teacher, and I'm not good at it. I thought we'd have a real teacher by now."

She went to the front door, then stood holding the jamb and looking out through the dust. She remembered wanting to see no more rain. *What a stupid wish that had been.*

"Where is Mr. Cosgrove?" asked Alice.

"He's taken the latest of my essays to the *Tribune*. This is my third try to get an article accepted, but I doubt we'll fare any better than the last two attempts. I just haven't the talent for essays."

"You sound bothered."

"I know I shouldn't complain," Katina said. "I've a place to sleep, thanks to Madame Jocelyn. I've work mending dresses for her, so there's a bit of money coming in. We have this theater for Homeplace, and only twice has someone tried to break in, and the only damage done was a couple of splintered shutters. Children who have never set foot in a schoolhouse are learning a little, in spite of me. There are fewer people going to bed hungry at night."

"And," added Becky, "John Brandermill has at last

been arrested for the murder of his wife, and sits in the jail at the courthouse as we speak."

"Yes," said Katina. "But still—" She stopped.

*But still*, she thought. In spite of the growing conviction she felt for this place and the growing trust she was gaining in other people, she felt as if something were missing.

"It's Mr. Cosgrove, ain't it?" asked Alice.

Katina turned around. "Hmmm?"

"You're glum because Mr. Cosgrove won't pay you no mind, not like a man to a woman, that is. I can tell you like him. And I think he likes you, too. But he ain't gonna say nothing."

"I—" began Katina. Alice was right. Ever since that night four weeks ago when Katina had revealed herself as a woman, Russell had continued to be friendly, but he had also begun to keep his distance. They had worked side by side for many weeks, laughing and fuming over the creation of Homeplace, eating meals and working on the essays. At times they had shared a smile that seemed a little sweeter than usual, or they had brushed hands while working, and she had felt a shiver of expectation and thought he had, too. But for some reason, he never let on.

"Tell me," said Katina, sitting down beside Becky and picking up a handful of peas to shell. "Why won't he say anything? He isn't shy by any means."

"Shy ain't the problem," said Becky. "It's something else. It's—" And then she stopped, nodded at the door, and whispered, "It's him."

Adam MacPherson stood in the doorway, grinning

broadly and holding a battered book in his hands. "Hello, ladies! Simple Parker's wife gave me a geology book her son used to study, and I thought you could use it for the school." He came in and sat down at the table. He had obviously brushed his hair and tried to scrub the dust from his face.

"Hello, Adam," said Alice and Becky in unison.

"Hello," said Katina. She wasn't sure what she thought of Adam anymore. When he had found out she was a girl, he had immediately banned her from performing with the theater troupe. No women, he'd always said, and he hadn't changed his mind. Katina was angry at first, but her anger had cooled because her attention was on Homeplace and the essay. As time went on, Adam had begun to come around several times a day. Katina sensed he had taken a fancy to her, in spite of the fact that she never did anything to encourage him.

"Where is everybody?" asked Adam.

"Are you looking for someone?" asked Alice. "Mr. Cosgrove ain't here."

"Good, I mean, I wasn't looking for anyone," Adam said. "I just brought the book. And I wanted to remind you that Pip, Chadwick, and I are performing tonight. Make sure the place is cleaned and empty by six."

"We always do," said Alice.

Adam scratched at his eyebrow. "Could I speak with you a moment, Katina?"

"Now isn't convenient," she answered. "The women's society will be here any moment."

"Ah, well, then. Later, I hope." He stood and said,

"You are taking good care of my theater, thank you. Good day." He tipped his well-worn hat and walked outside.

"That is why Mr. Cosgrove gives you a wide berth," said Becky. "He believes Adam is courting you."

"But he isn't! I don't want him to. What can I do?"

Alice and Becky suddenly grinned, but said nothing.

The Homeplace Women's Society gathered twice a week at two o'clock—a handful of scarred, dirty, yet hopeful ladies of all ages who wanted very much to learn reading, arithmetic, and a bit of etiquette. Today, seven women and their ten babies came. As the women settled themselves on benches and around the table, the babies placed gently on the floor in their blankets, Alice made an announcement. "Miss Katina has helped us a lot, teachin' us things about books and manners. But today it's time to help her!"

The women nodded, and Katina thought, *Oh, dear. What does Alice have in mind?*

The girls from the Stick Saloon called it a "coming-out party," and Becky whispered in Katina's ear that once Mr. Cosgrove saw how fixed up and pretty she was, he would have to make a bid for her in spite of Adam. For the next hour, as Alice combed Katina's chin-length hair into a semblance of curls, and as Becky presented Katina with a bright blue bonnet with a daisy pinned to the side, the women took turns offering advice about men.

"Don't laugh too loud, men don't like that!" said one.

"Don't tell them what to do," said another.

"Smile a lot."

"Don't nag."

"Sit up straight. A man isn't looking for a woman with a bad back."

Katina watched the eyes of the women light up with the thought that they were giving something of value back to her, in payment for the lessons and the food over the past months. Some of the advice about kindness and understanding was good. Other advice she shrugged off. But all the comments were appreciated, because she knew they were given with good wishes.

Then Becky opened a little bag she had with her and began to apply rouge in spite of Katina's protests.

"Oh, give me a chance!" said Becky. "I know what I'm doing!" And so Katina sat still as Becky rubbed and painted.

When Becky was done, there were "Ahhs" from some of the ladies and frowns from others.

"Who has a looking glass?" asked Katina.

No one did, but there was a barrel of water behind the theater, and all the ladies trooped out after Katina as she went to see her reflection in the water.

"You're going to love it!" said Alice.

Katina looked in the water. She recoiled.

Her cheeks were brilliant red, as were her lips. Her eyebrows had been blackened, and her eyelids were smudged with a sickly shade of orange.

"You look like one of the girls at the Stick!" said Becky with a huge grin of approval.

*Exactly!* thought Katina. *I have got to get out of this*

*gracefully. I can't bear to imagine what anyone seeing me on the street like this would think!*

"I appreciate your trouble," Katina said as she and the women went back inside. "But it itches so! Let me wipe off some. Perhaps my skin would need to get used to such beauty treatments before I could wear so much."

"All right," said Alice reluctantly. She handed Katina a handkerchief, and as the women collected their children and bid each other good-bye, Katina went back out to the water barrel and scrubbed her face vigorously. It didn't take long to remove most of the color, but a touch of it remained on her cheeks and lips, and Katina found the small amount pleasing. With the new bonnet and fresh look, she wondered if Russell might truly notice, and forget anything he suspected of Adam MacPherson.

"I'm running to Mrs. Savini's house," Katina told Alice, who had come outside to draw water for the upcoming meal. "She said she had a pig's head for us. I won't be long. I know you have to be back at the Stick shortly."

Mrs. Savini was an elderly widow who lived in a shack a block away. Her tiny house was falling down around her ears, she never could keep her pigs in their pens, and twice she'd been knocked on the head by men who had broken into her home, looking for something of value and finding nothing. Yet when she had heard about Homeplace, she had made a point of finding ways to help.

Katina walked briskly along the bright, dusty street,

wondering if she really looked pretty, wondering how many people would show up for the meal today and how many would be turned away, wondering if she should make one last visit to the Monroes and let them know she would visit them no longer, wondering so many things that she didn't realize someone was following her until she heard her name.

"Katina?"

She looked back. It was Adam, holding his hat.

"Adam! What do you want?"

He smiled. "You look different. You look pretty."

"Oh," she quipped, "and I usually don't look pretty?"

Adam came closer, his fingers fumbling with the hat. "That's not what I meant. I like the bonnet and the daisy. Are you trying to impress someone?"

"Alice was having fun, that's all."

Adam's face became serious. "I never went back to the work site after bringing the book today. I waited by the pawn shop, hoping to talk to you alone."

"Simple Parker is going to be furious."

"I'm not going to work for him anymore. I've tried out for a position with Steward Grand Theatre. I've got a good chance there, small roles at first, but it's what I've wanted. Fame, remember? And soon, fortune!"

"I thought you wanted to own your own theater."

"I have to be realistic. The MacPherson Theater is a dream that hasn't come true. I'll be accepted among great actors at Steward. Performing for the well-to-do! Katina, you are an excellent actor—actress—whatever. You don't need to be teaching ruffians, sewing for saloon girls. I could get you an audition! Maybe they would look at your plays. We could have a wonderful time, out of the slum."

"I don't understand, Adam."

"Yes, you do," said Adam. He took Katina's arm. "I have become fond of you. I think you feel the same. Look how you've fancied yourself up for me!" And he suddenly kissed her, a kiss that was passionate and insistent. A kiss that made her gasp and jerk away in horror.

And then she saw him standing behind Adam, holding her essay in his fist and staring aghast at the two of them through the bright sunlight that sparkled off the windows of the roadside shops.

Russell.

# 12

"Let me go!" said Katina, pushing Adam away. "What do you think you are doing?"

Adam looked stunned. "Katina," he mumbled. "I'm sorry, I . . . I thought there was no reason to hide my feelings now that I know you feel the same."

"But I don't!" she cried. "I don't care for you that way. And how dare you kiss me?"

"I didn't mean to offend you, Katina. Believe me, it's the last thing I meant to do, but I thought . . ."

Katina looked behind Adam again, but Russell was no longer there. *No, oh, no, this didn't happen. He didn't see us kissing!*

But clearly he had. And he was gone.

"Just go away, Adam," Katina cried. "Leave me alone. I'm sorry you feel misled, but I'm your friend, nothing more. Now, I need to fetch a pig's head!"

Adam gave her one last, confused look, then stalked off down the street. Katina counted her breaths, trying to compose herself. *I can't let him think I am in love with Adam*, she thought. *Forget the pig's head!*

With that, she gathered her skirts and raced back to the theater. Alice and Becky were standing at the stoves, heating water for the vegetables and pig's head. On the table behind them lay Katina's essay.

"Where's the head?" asked Alice.

"I don't have it!" said Katina. "Where's Russell?"

"He left. Was only here a second," said Becky. "Said he had boot-blacking to do and didn't know when he'd be back, and requested you kindly handle today's meal on your own."

"Oh, God." Katina dropped to a bench. "I can't believe this!"

"What's the matter?"

Katina shook her head. She didn't want to explain. It was personal, and it was embarrassing. It hurt her heart too much to speak of it. She didn't dare put the words on her lips.

"Do you want me to get the pig's head?" asked Alice.

"If you don't mind," Katina managed. "I'm so shaky I don't think I can walk at the moment."

Alice left, and Becky sat with her arm around Katina. "I don't know what's bothering you," she said. "But I know that whatever it is, whatever ghost is chasing you, it is always best if you turn right around and chase it back. You never win, running away. It's like in a dream, when a monster's coming? You turn to him and yell and he disappears."

Katina nodded. She knew Becky was right. She felt

a surprising surge of courage. "I should go right now. Can you stay a bit longer? No more than an hour, I promise! I won't let you be late for work."

"If it's that important, then go," said Becky.

"I will be back, I promise," said Katina. "Thank you, Becky!" She ran for the door.

"It's about Mr. Cosgrove, ain't it?" Becky called after her. Katina said, "Yes!"

*Where can he be?* she wondered, holding her skirts and running down the middle of the gritty, potholed street. *What is he thinking? Where does he shine shoes? In the business district, I know that much, but where exactly? There are so many streets!*

"Miss Monroe!" It was Bruce, running behind her, waving his arms. "Where you off to? Is there a fire?"

"No," said Katina. "Bruce, you shine shoes with Mr. Cosgrove on occasion. Tell me, where does he work?"

"All over," said Bruce, keeping pace with her. "Around State Street and Madison."

"Isn't there a main place?"

"Well, there *is* this maple tree . . ."

He told her the location of the tree, then asked if he could come, too. But she said, "Not this time. Listen to me, stay here. Do you hear me?"

"That's not fair!" he whined.

"I'm sorry, but you must do as I say!" And without waiting for any more arguments, she ran off, hoping he wasn't following. He wasn't.

State Street was clogged with traffic, both on the street and the sidewalks. There were many trees along the street, as well, but Katina pushed her way through the crowds, seeking the one near Mrs. Archer's Millinery. Her bonnet strings had come loose, and her hat slid off her head and bounced at her neck. She yanked it free and gripped it in her fist.

*Please be there, Russell! If I don't find you soon I may lose my nerve!*

She saw the millinery up ahead, with three prim ladies standing outside the door. She worked her way past with quick apologies, and then spied the maple tree. The leaves were heavy and browning in the heat. And under the tree was a tall man in a white shirt with dark hair.

*Thank you, God!*

She jumped from the sidewalk to the street and grabbed the man by the elbow. "Russell!" The man glanced over his shoulder. He had a thick mustache, sideburns, and red pimples on his forehead. He gave Katina a look of disapproval from behind his spectacles.

"Watch who you touch!" he scowled.

"I'm sorry, sir, I was looking for the bootblack who often works beneath this tree."

"I've seen no bootblack. Now, go on about your business!"

Katina looked back and forth frantically. *What if he didn't go to shine shoes after all? What if he's decided to go away for a while? Would he do that to the people who needed him? Would he do that to me?*

"I don't know!" she said aloud, and a lady nearby, stepping into a horsecar with her small daughter, glanced at her as if she were touched in the head.

And then she saw a man polishing the boots of another man across the street in front of a lawyer's office. The bootblack was kneeling down, rubbing the leather with a brush, as the man stood over him, looking at his pocket watch. Katina crossed the road, dodging carriages and jumping horsecar tracks. The bootblack gave a final buff with the brush, stood, and took the coins handed him. He stuck the coins into his pocket and began to pack the wooden box as the gentleman left.

Katina said, "Sir, you do a fine polish."

Russell turned around and looked at her. She couldn't read his face. It was sweaty and red from the heat, but his eyes were steady. "Hello, there," he said. "Is there something wrong at Homeplace?"

"No," Katina said, realizing how out of breath she was now, and how it hurt to breathe.

"Did someone send you to get me?"

"No."

"Then what have you run all the way here for? Did you want to know about your essay, the one I took to the *Tribune?*"

"Well, yes, I do, but . . ."

"They rejected it."

"As I suspected," she said. "But that doesn't matter right now."

"No?"

"Russell," she began. *How to say this?* She felt her head spinning, but her feet were secure on the road. "What you saw earlier, I wanted to explain."

"Earlier?"

"With Adam."

"Oh, that," he said. The corners of his eyes looked pinched with hurt, though he kept it from his voice. "Why should you explain? It's none of my business. I must offer you congratulations, however. I didn't realize how much your feelings for each other had grown."

"Russell, don't say another word. Not one! And listen to me." She slowly unpinned the daisy from her bonnet and pressed it into his hand. He looked at the flower but didn't pull away. "I do not care for Adam. He is a friend, but I've misread his actions these many weeks. It took Becky and Alice to point out to me that he saw me as a potential sweetheart."

Russell said, "I thought that, too."

"I've been so busy becoming myself again that I was unaware of his behavior. I've loved writing the essay, even if it keeps failing. I've loved working at Homeplace, even though I'm not a very good teacher. I'm learning to trust, Russell! That's quite a change for me. If only you knew . . ." she stopped. *If you only knew the truth, Russell. But how can I say it when I don't know how you'll react?*

Russell's fingers squeezed hers around the flower, ever so slightly. "Knew what?" he asked.

"That . . . that it is you I love," she whispered.

Russell's fingers tightened more firmly. "Katina, what did you say?"

She looked him full in the face. "That it is you I love, Russell Cosgrove. And no other."

Russell's face lit up, and he dropped his polish box

to the ground. He took Katina's other hand in his and said, "Katina, how I've wanted to say that to you. I've longed to tell you how beautiful you are, how wonderful, and yet there was Adam. Always Adam, everywhere. And now you tell me it isn't him that you love?"

She shook her head. There were tears in her eyes and she didn't wipe them away.

"You tell me it is me," said Russell.

"Yes."

"And I love you, too," he said. "I love you!"

"But my essay is rejected!"

"I love you, but your essay is rejected!"

Katina laughed. And Russell swept her into his arms and spun her around on the edge of State Street, while passing lawyers and financiers and shipping magnates and ladies looked on disapprovingly, but it didn't matter, none of that mattered, because she loved him and he loved her and the world was bright and warm and so very, very new.

# 13

### Another Week With No Rain, Frolic Planned

The City Council has announced "Frolic by the Lake" for September 22, an event planned to take the minds of the citizens of Chicago off the dread, dry weather that has plagued us since July. Bands are scheduled to play, and there will be games of badminton and croquet.

Only four brief showers have rained on our city in the past month and a half, causing late summer crops to fail, rain barrels to go empty, and tempers to sour. Streets are dust bins, and the elderly have experienced a high rate of lung diseases due to the dryness. There have been more fires in our city than in the last year, with a report of 613 at this date. With heaven's help, there will come rain in the not-too-distant future. It would benefit us all.

— George Rainey, *Chicago Tribune*,
September 19, 1871

Adam MacPherson sold his theater at the end of September and told Russell and Katina that everything belonging to Homeplace had to be out by Monday, October ninth, when the new owner, a whiskey dealer, would move in. Russell suspected that the sale of the building had to do with Katina's rejection of Adam, and she agreed. Adam was hurt, and he'd gotten a job at the Grand Theater, and so was washing his hands of his old home and old friends. He'd even found room and board with another actor who lived on the North Side.

The last meal for the poor was served on Saturday afternoon. Becky wasn't there to help because she was at the Stick, in bed with a fever. But Alice had come early to help prepare for the crowd; she looked as pretty as she could in a green dress, as if the last dinner should be a celebration. Russell and Katina decided that Alice was right: the meal should be joyous. They sent Bruce off in search of flowers, instructing him to ask for flowers from the street vendor on Griswold, not to steal them, while Russell went to Sallee's Butcher Shop to beg some decent meat and Katina asked the pawn shop owner, Rolf Goltman, if he would play his fiddle.

Forty-three people were fed that afternoon, the

largest number ever, and there was purple larkspur in jars to brighten the room, German songs fiddled by Mr. Goltman, and an incredible meal of bacon, bread, cabbage, and apple pie. Men, women, and children sat at the large table, on the benches, on the floor, and outside at the side of the dusty street. They gobbled up the food, shared scraps with Stump, and tapped their feet to the music.

Side by side at the stove, Russell and Katina stood with their arms around each other. Russell struggled with mixed emotions. Homeplace, which had been open for only five months, was going to close down, with not a single acknowledgment by the *Chicago Tribune* or a bit of help from anyone with wealth. He wanted to continue the work, but he would have to start from scratch. And yet, here at this very moment were happy people, temporarily lifted from the drudgery of life. And here beside him, with her arm at his waist, was a beautiful, loving, intelligent woman.

Katina put her head against his arm and said, "Don't worry. We may not have a building, but we've got the furniture and other goods. Madame Jocelyn said we can store everything at the Stick until we find a new place."

Russell kissed the top of Katina's head. "We do what we can."

The celebration went on until nearly six in the evening, with Mr. Goltman getting wild on the fiddle and people dancing in the street. Although the autumn had been brutally dry and hot, energy rose from the crowd like butterflies to the sky. Katina and Russell danced, too, but Russell felt clumsy and whispered apologetically in her ear that gracefulness was not a family trait.

At long last, Russell told everyone that he had to lock the building. The music and the dancing stopped, and the men, women, and children faded away into the shadows of early evening.

Katina, Russell, and Alice cleaned the stove, swept the floor, then went out and locked the door. With the struggling Stump under one arm, Russell tugged the lock to make sure it was secure. He turned to find the two women with tears in their eyes.

"Oh," he said, pulling them both to him in a hug. "Nobody's died. We've lost nothing but our location."

They stood together for a long moment.

And then another woman's voice said, "Why, this is as lovely a sight as I've seen in a long time!"

The three pulled away from each other, and Russell stared at the lady in the tea cart who had spoken. She was dressed in satin, with her golden hair pinned up beneath a velvet cap. Her eyes were as green as Irish shamrocks. Both the driver and the pony stared ahead with proper disinterest.

"Rebecca," Russell said.

"Yes!" said Rebecca. She opened the door of the cart and stepped out, then carefully picked her way across the road. She took Russell's hand in hers. "Russell, I was so glad you wrote to me! The letter was so incredibly sweet. You know how I've missed you, our talks, our merriment, our walks. But, oh!" she glanced about, wrinkling her nose. "I did fear for my life coming here. Men shouting from doorways, making lewd comments! And look at you, so much worse for the wear. But don't worry, we're together again!"

Russell glanced at Katina. She was staring at the rich young woman with apprehension. He knew how bad this looked, how bad it sounded. He prayed Katina would understand once he had a chance to explain.

Clearing his throat, Russell introduced Katina and Alice, then handed Stump to Katina and said he needed a moment alone with Rebecca. Alice said she had to go to work, and Katina shrugged and said simply, "Whatever you need to do." Then she leaned against the theater door with the dog in her arms and her jaw set.

Russell and Rebecca walked to the corner of the street, then Russell said as calmly as possible, "Why did you come here?"

Rebecca dabbed her nose with her handkerchief, clearly uncomfortable with her surroundings. "You wrote me. You said you needed financial help to run this . . . this whatever you call it for the poor. You said you had tried to place an article about your work in the *Tribune* and were facing a long winter with little reserve. You hoped I would consider a donation in spite of our less than pleasant parting. Yet you expected me to send money to your parents' house without seeing you?"

Russell took a deep breath. "I wrote you for help," he said. "But I didn't mean to rekindle our relationship."

Rebecca touched his arm. "We can do both, Russell.

I've been graduated from Brickmeyer's now. I've not started my girls' school yet, but I could use your help. Here is my idea: I will help you with your poorhouse if you will help me start my girls' school."

"I can't."

"Why can't you?" She touched his cheek, and for a moment he remembered their first kiss, and how warm he'd felt. But he pulled her hand away and said, "If you won't help me without stipulations, then I must apologize for taking your time and ask you to leave."

Rebecca made a tsk sound, then said, "I admire your determination, Russell, but this is a phase you're in. I knew you liked to talk about social conditions, but I didn't think you really wanted to get this involved. No one wants to live in a place like this if they have a choice. I'm offering you a choice. You know where to find me." She called for her driver, climbed into the cart, and waved good-bye.

Russell walked back to Katina, who watched him with steady eyes. "She was an old friend," he said. "She only came to talk about supporting Homeplace."

"You wrote her for help?"

"Well, yes, I wasn't going to, but . . ."

"You shared walks, you shared *merriment* with her?"

"It was a long time ago. I thought she might help. We have so little money. You do understand?"

Katina put Stump down. "She's very beautiful."

"Yes. But you are more beautiful."

"Do you love her?"

Russell knew he couldn't lie. "I did. But no more."

"I see."

"Listen," Russell said, taking a breath. "It's a fine evening. Why don't we take a walk, or even catch a ride on a horsecar? No one needs us tonight. Is there someplace you would like to go, someplace that would make you feel better, to take our minds off things? Let's take a stroll and clear our heads."

"I suppose," said Katina. But her voice was cool. *Hopefully*, Russell thought, *a nice walk will help us both forget Rebecca's visit.* He held his arm out for her to take, but she walked with her hands at her side.

After depositing Stump in Russell's apartment, they meandered out of the slum through the business district. They said little to each other, but Russell knew that at times silence could be healing. He knew he sometimes talked too much, rambling on when quiet was needed. When she was ready to talk, he would talk.

By the time they found themselves on Michigan Avenue, the sky was dark and filled with stars. A warm southwestern breeze tugged at their clothes. On the vast water, ship lights bobbed like fireflies. Couples and families were out to enjoy the evening, strolling along the lane with its red- and yellow-leaved trees.

Katina suddenly stopped and pointed at a stone mansion within a stone wall. "There is my family," she said, "though they deny it. I've come here every other Sunday with a letter, and every other Sunday have been turned away."

Russell nodded. Beside him, Katina began to tremble. He put his arm around her waist, and she did not pull away.

"A year and a half of trying," she said, staring at the

house. "It is rather pathetic, don't you think? It's like a crazy woman, like a lunatic in an asylum, beating her head on the wall."

"It's not crazy, wanting something out of reach. How else would we ever gain something if we didn't try?"

She turned abruptly, and walked across the wide street to where a short, wooden pier extended into the lake between the fenced yards of two stately mansions. A rowboat was tethered to the pier, and it rolled with the waves. Katina climbed onto the pier and walked to the end, her skirt blowing in the wind off the water, her hands outstretched as if trying to catch something she desperately needed and desperately wanted. She tilted her head back, like a drowning woman trying to find her breath.

Russell followed her, and when he had reached her, he took her upturned chin in his hands and said, "They don't know you or want you. But I do."

Katina's trembling grew stronger. But her voice was clear, "I need to let the Monroes go. There must be freedom in letting go."

"I think there is," Russell said. "We must let go of many things to move on. We have to let go of the old Homeplace to be open to the possibility of a new, better safe haven."

Katina whispered, "It's hard."

"It is." He brought his face to hers, he ran his cheek along the soft curve of her nose, her cheek, her forehead. He took in the wonderful smell of her hair and skin. She sighed, almost inaudibly.

*Writing Rebecca for money was grasping at straws*, he told himself. *But after the* Tribune *rejected all of Katina's essays, I panicked. But no more. I will work, I will move forward, and I won't look back.*

"I won't look back," he said. His lips found Katina's and she responded urgently, salty tears beginning to roll and mingle with the kiss. His hands moved from her face to her neck, and he kissed the gentle spot of her throat. Katina's fingers found his hair and caressed it almost painfully, then pushed his suspenders from his shoulders. Her mouth sought his again, and the warmth and passion drew a moan from his lips. She whispered, "There must be freedom in letting go."

He closed his eyes as she feathered her fingers along his arms, pausing at the scar left from the knifing. Every fiber in his body awakened, longing to be touched by her.

"Love me," she said.

"I do."

She touched his eyelids and he looked at her. "Love me," she repeated.

"I will," he answered. His hands slid to her shoulders and she leaned into him, pressing against him with the whole of her body, and he pressed into her. Her breathing was faster now. The pier beneath his feet seemed to sway. Katina knelt on the pier, bringing Russell down with her. She looked up at him and what he saw in the sparkling starlight was the most beautiful sight in his life. "Love me," she whispered.

And he did. And she loved him back, fiercely, their kisses saying everything their hearts longed to say.

Morning came with a first hint of blue at the horizon across the lake. Waterbirds hovered around fishing boats that had gone out early for Sunday's catch. Katina and Russell, who had fallen asleep together, unlocked from each other, bringing on a cool rush of air.

Katina rubbed her neck and said, "I have to admit I slept better last night than I have in months in the attic at the Stick. There was no fighting from below, no breaking glass, no Madame Jocelyn in a tantrum." She looked over at Russell, feeling a rush of awkwardness, hoping to see in his eyes the same love she had seen in them the night before.

And the love was there. The blue eyes regarded her with awe, respect, and love. Katina felt her heart swell with wonder and joy.

They walked down Michigan Avenue, and Russell bought the two of them breakfast in a small restaurant near the Government Pier. They savored the bacon, eggs, toast, and oatmeal with molasses, even as Katina protested mildly that he'd spent several days' worth of his earnings as a bootblack.

It was the talk on State Street on the way home that first caught their attention, and then the gray cloud hanging in the air to the west. They caught bits of conversation from people on the sidewalks. "Huge, did you see?" "All night!" "Such a shame!"

"Worst fire in the history of this city," one gentleman was saying to another on the steps of a church as they held on to their hats in the wind. "With our city's alarm system and water mains, I'm surprised it got as bad as it did. Bunch of slovenly firemen on that poor side of town. Immigrants, you know."

Russell stopped and said, "Excuse me, sirs. What fire are you talking about?"

The two well-dressed men gave Russell a disdainful perusal, then one said, "Where have you been, New York? Last night there was a fire on the West Side, over where the lumberyards and paper factories are. Burned four blocks around Jackson Street. Nearly leaped the river, and it took the firefighters sixteen hours to put it out."

"Yes," said the other man as he put the tip of a match to his cigar. "Quite a spectator event. We rode over there last night, watched from the Madison Street Bridge." He laughed as if it was nothing more than a curiosity.

"Heard drunks over on a block of Fifth Avenue went crazy last night, too," said the first man. "Set a few of their own fires. Burned a shop, another place or two. Like animals, riled up by the excitement. But at least," he added with a wink to his partner, "the fire stayed where it belonged and didn't bother the finer neighborhoods."

"Pompous imbeciles," said Russell as he grabbed Katina's hand and they quickened their pace for home.

"Fires on Fifth Avenue?" Katina said. "I wonder where? I wonder what kind of damage?"

Russell didn't answer, but something in the painful beating of his heart told him they wouldn't like what they saw when they got there.

They could smell the smoke from two blocks away, and there were still citizens moving up Quincy Street to the river to have a look at the damage on the other side. But it was the damage on their own block that made Russell and Katina stare in disbelief. They stood at the corner, hands over their noses against the sharp bite of smoke, staring at the spot where the MacPherson Theater had been. The walls were blackened and had caved inward, dumping the shingled roof inside. The left side of the pawn shop next door was burned away, and Mr. Goltman was in the road, wringing his hands. Several children Russell didn't know were digging through the smoldering wreckage with sticks.

"Do you see this?" Mr. Goltman wailed. "The fire last night on the West Side was an accident. But this wasn't! This was intentional."

Russell stared at the charred cavern that had been Homeplace. Inside were all the books and furniture and clothing that they owned, everything they were going to store and then use to start again. Gone.

"It wasn't an accident?" Katina managed.

Mr. Goltman shook his head.

"Someone set it?"

The man nodded. "Heard a man called Brandermill got out of jail couple days ago, found innocent of killing his wife. Went on a binge last night with his buddies, and tried to discover who told on him. Word this morning is that he found the undertaker who buried the wife, and that the undertaker described a boy who nobody's seen in months and a tall man.

Brandermill asked around and got the idea that the man was you, Mr. Cosgrove."

Russell could barely speak. "He came after me?"

"Yes! Thinks you did it, but I don't want to know if that's the truth or not, so don't tell me! But he burned this stable and Mr. Sallee's butcher shop, hoping you were upstairs, sleeping. Fire engines came, kept the fire from destroying other buildings, but it's done."

*The shop? God, no!* Russell pushed the pawn shop dealer aside and raced to the end of the block. Mr. and Mrs. Sallee were sitting on a pair of burned chairs in the middle of the road, surrounded by an odd assortment of items they'd been able to get outside before the shop collapsed in flames. Mrs. Sallee was crying, rocking back and forth, and Mr. Sallee was staring at the remains with fury in his eyes, as if he could resurrect it all with sheer will. When he saw Russell and Katina, the butcher jumped to his feet and swung his fists at them. "It was *you* he was after! He wanted you dead. Now see? See what your being charitable has accomplished? Nothing but bad!"

"I did not have John Brandermill arrested!" Russell shouted, pushing the butcher away. "But I would have done it if someone else hadn't! My intentions are to do right!"

"The road to hell is paved with good intentions!"

"I never believed that!" Then Russell turned and looked into the burned, stinking maw that had once been a shop and his home. "Is there nothing left?" he asked as Katina held his arm.

"I don't think so," whispered Katina. She was shaking, her hands clenched. "And Stump was in there! Poor little Stump!"

Suddenly, Russell climbed into the black, twisted wreckage and began digging. Splinters bit his fingers; still-hot fragments of wood singed his palms.

"What are you looking for?" asked Katina. "Russell, it's all gone!"

"No, I won't let it be! There is something I must find. It will be a miracle if I find it, but it must be here! Just one thing!" His heart thundered with rage, grief, and frustration, his hands clawed for a recognizable remnant. He dug through burned bits of meat, wet, ashy scraps of clothes and curtains, broken jars and pottery, an upturned cookstove, a smoldering shoe.

Katina watched silently from the road. Mrs. Sallee continued to cry, and Mr. Sallee said he was off to have a drink at the Stick, there was nothing for him anymore.

And then, beneath an upturned slab of smoking wood that had been part of his desk, he found it.

"*Yes,*" he whispered.

"What is it?"

He held the Bible, still intact, to his chest and climbed back out to the road. "I've found it," he said in wonder. "This precious book, and all that is inside."

Katina took the book from him. "A sign of hope . . ." she said uncertainly. "A place to start."

And then her face went hard, and she stared at the road. Several envelopes had fluttered from the pages. She stooped to pick one up. "Oh, Russell . . ." she began.

"No, Katina, let me explain," said Russell. *How could I have forgotten they were in there?*

Katina glanced up at him, and the look was a lance in his soul. "These are her letters," she said slowly. "Rebecca's letters, aren't they?"

"Yes," said Russell. "But—"

"You said, 'This precious book, and all that is inside.' You had hoped to find her letters unharmed. They meant that much to you."

"No, Katina."

"*She* meant that much to you." Katina's eyes were brimming, but her words were controlled.

Russell reached for her, but she pulled away. "Don't you trust me?" he demanded. He knew his words sounded harsh, but he was so tired, so angry, so defeated. Couldn't she see what had happened? It was all gone, burned into nothing. "It wasn't the letters I had hoped to find." He took the Bible from her, and quickly flipped through the pages. *It must still be in here!* he thought. *Where is it?*

He looked up to see Katina backing away, holding her hands out in resignation. "I trusted you. Completely."

"Katina!"

"I'm going," she said simply. "I don't want to talk now, I don't want to be with you. I need to be alone. I don't understand what this means, Russell, and it hurts too much to consider. But you agreed there is freedom in letting go. Perhaps there is freedom from heartache!"

"Katina, it's you I love! That's all there is to understand."

"I need to be alone," she said, holding up a hand as if to stop him. "Don't follow me!" She turned and stalked off, her head defiantly high.

"I am going to see my parents on De Koven, then!" he called after her. "In case you want to know."

She turned the corner without looking back.

"In case you want to know," he repeated to the empty space she had filled just a moment ago. He sat down beside Mrs. Sallee and handed her the Bible. "You may want this more than I do," he said. "I pray you and your husband find peace. I cannot imagine at this moment that there is any for me."

She looked at the Bible in her lap, sniffed loudly, and opened the cover. "I can't read," she confessed.

Russell reached over and took out what had been stuck to the inside of the front cover. It was the pressed daisy Katina had given him on the day she first said she loved him. It was what he had meant when he had said there was something precious inside, not Rebecca's rambling missives.

For a moment he thought of chasing after Katina, but he knew her temper. He also knew that he, too, was angry, because she hadn't trusted him and had immediately thought the worst.

All was destroyed. His home. His dreams. His sweet little puppy. His true love. Her trust.

And so he took the dried daisy, put it into his shirt pocket, rubbed the soot from his hands as best he could, and began the long walk to the West Side across the river.

## 14

It was always difficult to tell what time it was from the windowless attic bedroom in the Stick Saloon. Although most of the rowdy drinking and gambling was two floors down, it was constant and loud, as raucous at noontime as it was at 2 A.M., breaking only when Madame Jocelyn flew into a temper and kicked everybody out.

Katina had fallen asleep not long after leaving Russell at the burned-down shop, then climbing the narrow steps to the attic from the second floor and dropping onto her cot in a fit of tears. *It cannot be worse than this*, she had thought. *Homeplace is destroyed. What I had with Russell is destroyed. My heart is broken. There is nothing left to lose.* She had cried, then cried again, until sleep pulled at her and took her into its soft, motherly arms.

But then Alice was at the door calling, "Katina! You have to get up and see it!"

Katina opened her eyes, blinking. It was pitch-dark, with a slice of light from Alice's lantern beneath the door. "What is it? I really want to be alone."

"It's started again," the girl said. "We're all going to the bridge to watch. Don't you want to come, too?"

"What's started?"

"Another fire. On the West Side. This one is worse than the one yesterday!"

Alice didn't wait for Katina to get up. She opened the door, and the light startled Katina to full consciousness, causing her to blink madly.

"Are you sure it's not the smoldering from Saturday's fire that looks like a new fire?" Katina asked.

"Can't you hear the bells?"

And through the thin walls of the attic, Katina could indeed hear the clanging of the distant courthouse bell, and the fainter, accompanying sound of church bells. This was a true alarm.

"There's always a fire somewhere, Alice. I have more things to worry about than someone's burning toolshed."

"This is much worse! I looked outside already!"

"What time is it?"

"Quarter after ten or so. Come on!"

"What about Becky?"

"She's still sick in bed. She'll be fine. We'll be back when the fire's out and she'll never know we're gone."

Katina slipped out of her nightgown and into her dress and shoes.

Downstairs, the saloon was empty except for

Madame Jocelyn, who sat at a table smoking a cigar. "They've all run off and left me!" snarled the white-haired woman. "Think it's more of a lark to watch a fire than play cards with me? Fine, I'll shut the place down for a few hours, see how they like that!"

"We'll be right back," Alice offered tentatively, then dragged Katina outside by the hand.

In the street, the wind had picked up, and the crowd was clutching skirt hems, jacket collars, and caps, pushing westward toward the river, their chatter anxious and loud. The boardinghouses and saloons lining the street had lanterns blazing in windows, making the road seem nearly as bright as day.

"I heard someone say there was nine blocks gone already!" shouted one woman to another as Katina and Alice stepped onto the rutted road. "What do you think we've done for God to pass such judgment?"

"Ain't judgment," said the other woman. "It's this dry weather and this wind! All the water in the world can't put out a strong wind!"

"Nine blocks!" said Katina, grabbing Alice's elbow. Russell was on the West Side with his family. He surely couldn't be in the path of the fire! "Do you think that's true? I can't imagine such a blaze!"

"Me, either," said Alice. She and Katina picked up their pace. "Let's get to the Madison Street Bridge. We can best see from there."

A man bumped into Katina, and then another, giving no apologies but pushing around and ahead. The others in the crowd seemed oblivious to the shoving. There was entertainment ahead, regardless of how grim, and they wanted to get to the river faster than the others to find a good place from which to watch.

"Look at that sky!" said Alice.

Across the river and to the south, the sky was pulsing orange and red. Flames could be seen intermittently, leaping upward in red fingers somewhere beyond the remains of lumberyards and factories that were still smoking from Saturday's blaze. Smoke billowed.

*It looks like war,* Katina thought as she and Alice stumbled onto the end of the bridge and stopped, unable to go farther because of the crowd. *It looks like what the renegades did. It looks like Merrifield, magnified over and over!*

Madison Street Bridge was already crammed with people pressed against each other, clutching the railings, shouting and pointing at the sight. Children squealed, laughed, and ran about as if they were at a party. Police officers had placed themselves in the midst of the commotion, some on foot and others on horseback, but they seemed as curious as the rest about what was happening over on the West Side and did little to deter the crowd. Rooftops along the river's edge were lined with people who had climbed up to watch. The wind-churned water of the river reflected the terrible inferno to the southwest, its waves shimmering with red and gold. Barges and small steamboats moved as quickly as they could up the river, trying to escape what could be their doom if the fire wasn't halted. Although this bridge, like the others that spanned the river, was capable of being cranked and turned away from the banks until it was parallel to the river in order to let larger ships pass, it remained in place across the water as the curious crammed onto it. Sailboats and other tall vessels would have to wait until the bridge was turned to get out.

"Does anyone know where the fire started?" Katina shouted. No one answered. "Where did it start, please, I must know!" A woman turned and stared at her, then passed the question up the line along the bridge. A minute later, an answer was passed back. "Someone said Clinton Street. Someone else said De Koven!"

Katina's knees buckled. It felt as though someone had punched her in the chest. Alice caught her beneath her arms. "Katina, don't you faint on me!"

"Russell's over there," Katina said. She drew in all her strength and pushed herself upward, locking her shaking legs beneath her. "Russell's visiting his family! They live on De Koven!"

"Sweet God, do you think he's dead?" Alice asked in a hushed, horrified whisper.

"Don't say that! Don't even think that!" She looked ahead at the thick crowd on the bridge. It would be hard to get through, but she had to do it. *I have to find Russell.* She had to make sure he was safe, that he was not in danger. And she had to tell him she was sorry, so very sorry! She knew the letters didn't mean anything to him, not really.

*I've been distrustful for too long*, she thought. *Yet he's been so caring, so patient. I have to tell him I was wrong not to hear him out today! I have to tell him that I do love him.*

*I have to find him!* "Alice," she said. "I've got to go find him!"

But Alice gave her a sharp shake of the elbow. "No! It's too dangerous!"

"It doesn't matter!" Katina turned sideways, and tried to push her way through the gaping crowds, but angry people shoved her out of the way. *I love him,* she thought. *He said the letters meant nothing, and I believe he was telling the truth. If I had not been so stiff-necked, he would still have been on Fifth Street, where it is safe. It is my fault he is in danger now!* One fat, sweaty man lifted Katina and dumped her back. "I have to get through to the other side!" she cried, but no one seemed to care.

"Katina!" came a small voice. It was Bruce Charles, not far from Katina, clutching the side of the bridge. He was grinning broadly. "Ain't it exciting?"

"It's not exciting!" she shouted. "It's dreadful! All those poor people, and Russell in the middle of it!"

"Russell's over there?"

"Yes, and I have to find him!"

"I'll go, too!"

"No, Bruce!" said Katina, but of course, Bruce didn't listen. He let go of the railing and grabbed Katina's hand. "Give us room!" he said to those around him. "Lady with consumption here, let her through!"

The people nearby gave Katina a disgusted stare, then stepped away far enough for the two of them to move forward. "Got consumption, get out of the way!" said Bruce. People moved against each other to let them pass. Katina added effect by coughing loudly.

*We'll get over the bridge,* Katina thought, *then keep to*

*the riverbank as best we can, climbing grain elevators and factory fences when we have to! De Koven is south, I know. We will find him!*

"I think I see St. Paul's steeple," yelled one man on the bridge. "Yes, that's up, burning like a torch!"

"Incredible!" shouted another.

*How could anyone think watching this is sport?* thought Katina. *It's horrific!*

There was the clang of fire engine bells coming from the east, and the people on the bridge crushed themselves together to let them pass.

"It must be a dreadful fire, for sure," said Bruce. "Extra engines from our side goin' over to help!"

Three horse-drawn steam engines from South Side fire departments clambered onto the bridge, forcing their way through the spectators. Clouds of steam and cinders hissed from the engines' huge boiler stacks, and a fireman running alongside shouted at the people through his brass speaking trumpet. "Get off the bridge! We are needed, space is needed, let us through!"

Some of the crowd backed up, although many people just pressed themselves together more tightly, stubbornly keeping their places. Katina could no longer move forward, the crowd was too tight.

Someone cried, "It's crossed to South Side!"

And it had. The wind had blown ash and chunks of flaming buildings across the water. About a quarter mile down the river, flames could now be seen on both sides. The curious expressions of the spectators began to fade as they realized what was happening. If the wind kept up, their homes would be next. There were gasps now in the crowd, and some women screamed.

"Bruce!" Katina said. "I'm going across on the rail."

"You aren't!"

"Yes," said Katina. "I'll be careful."

Slowly, she pulled herself up onto the wide, flat bridge railing and clung to it on hands and knees. All she had to do was crawl to the other side, about twenty yards away, and not look down. The water was thirty feet or more below, and she could not swim. *I'll make it*, she told herself, her heart pounding. *I've got good balance, I'm strong!*

Suddenly a fourth steam engine crossed the bridge, its horses snorting madly, and the crowd caused it to career off its path. The side of the engine struck the rail and scraped along it for a moment. Katina looked back and was face-to-face with a terrified fireman at the reins. He reached out for her at the last second, but it was too late.

The impact threw her knees out from under her. Then she was falling over the side, her arms flailing, her hands grasping nothing but air, until she struck the water with a force that knocked her breath from her body, and she was sucked down into the cold and the wet and the black.

# 15

Russell had gone for a walk Sunday evening in his old neighborhood, after having a meal with his parents in their cottage on De Koven and telling them about the destruction of Homeplace but not about the way he and Katina had parted. His mother had given him an extra serving of squash to make him feel better. His father had taken him out back to show him how the dry weather had killed his crop of pumpkins, then had put his arm around his son's shoulder and said, "You come from strong stock. Our family has always survived whatever has been put in our way."

Russell had thanked his father for the encouragement, but he had not felt encouraged. Not bothering with a lantern, he left his parents' house at nine o'clock in his canvas coat and strolled east along the dark, dusty street, past the ramshackle cottages with their unpainted fences and cluttered yards. It was obvious from the dark windows that most of the neighbors were in bed. The wind was steady from the west, blowing grit and dry leaf crumbs in Russell's face.

He sat on the edge of the wooden sidewalk outside the O'Learys' house, pushed up the sleeves of his coat, and took the pressed daisy from his pocket. He looked at it, and then at the hands that held it. Hands had a great deal of power, power to help, power to hurt. The way he had left Katina this afternoon was wrong. Not going after her to show her the flower and to assure her of his love had been cruel. She'd been hurt so much in her life. He wanted to be part of her healing, not part of her pain. Although the night was warm, regret ran cold beneath his skin.

"Tomorrow morning," he said as he put the flower back into his pocket. "I shall return to the Stick. I'm going to tell her I'm sorry, and ask her to marry me."

"What's that?" came a voice nearby. He looked down the road to see James Dalton, a neighbor, sitting on the walk in front of his house, smoking his pipe.

"Just woolgathering," said Russell.

"Mmm, hmmm," said James, and went back to his pipe.

Russell looked up at the leaves flying over his head like silent ghosts. *Such a thought, marriage.* He would not have fathomed such a thing was possible six months ago. *But now it seems right. To have her and hold her.* He would have someone to rejoice with, someone to hold and cherish when the world turned harsh.

"If she will forgive me," he said quietly. "Dear God, please let her forgive me!"

He smelled it at the same moment he heard the

shout behind him, "Fire, fire!" Russell jumped to his feet and turned to see a tongue of flame licking out from the window of the barn behind the O'Learys' house. And then Peg Leg Sullivan, a neighbor with a wooden leg, was running across the O'Leary yard and pointing. "The barn! It's gone up! We have to wake everyone! I'll get the cows!"

As Peg Leg hobbled behind the O'Leary house and yanked open the door to the burning shed, Russell took the O'Learys' front steps two at a time and pounded on the door. He knew from his mother that this part of the house was rented to Patrick McLaughlin, and Russell could hear the McLaughlin family inside, singing and talking. "Fire's in the barn!" he yelled. "McLaughlin, there's fire out back! Get out!"

The singing stopped and Mr. McLaughlin called, "What?"

"Fire!" repeated Russell. Waiting no longer, he jumped from the porch and was joined by James Dalton. They raced to the side door, which was the entrance to the O'Learys' part of the house. "Fire in your barn, wake up!" shouted James through the shuttered window.

"Get out now!" cried Russell, banging on the door.

From the barn, Peg Leg emerged, without his wooden leg, clutching the neck of a wild-eyed calf. Smoke and flame billowed out behind him, and flames had broken through the roof. Sparks rode the wind to the roof of the O'Leary house and James Dalton's yard next door. "Horse and cows are burned up!" Peg Leg shouted to Russell. "Lost my leg in a hole, couldn't stay to pull it out. This one's going to travel fast!"

Patrick O'Leary opened the door of his cottage and stared in horror at the burning barn and the shower of sparks. "Catherine!" he called into the house. "Get the children, there's fire!"

Neighbors had heard the shouting and were quick with buckets and pans of water from their wells and pumps. Women, children, men, and old people converged in the yard, tossing the water onto the barn, which was clearly past saving. The O'Learys' roof was smoldering now, and the dry grass in Mr. Dalton's yard had ignited. Russell joined the brigade from the O'Learys' well to the blaze, hauling up buckets full of water and passing them down the line. But he knew it was futile. There was no way citizens could stop this on their own. It was spreading too quickly. Embers blew from the Dalton yard, landed on the shed roof and dry garden next to it, and took hold.

"I'll alert the fire department!" Russell called.

"The nearest alarm box is at Bruno Goll's drugstore on Canal!" called Peg Leg as he tossed a bucket of water against the side of the O'Learys' house, where it sizzled worthlessly into steam.

A block away from the drugstore Russell met William Lee, who was returning from Canal Street, panting and wheezing. "I've gone about the alarm, if that's where you're running to," he said. "Mr. Goll wouldn't give me the alarm box key. Said he would telegraph the alarm himself. The engines should be here soon, I pray God!"

"He refused to give you the key?" Russell asked. This was odd. Citizens had the right to get the alarm box key and send the message to the central dispatch office at the courthouse themselves.

William nodded. "Mr. Goll seemed perturbed that I disturbed him. Woke him up, interrupted a game of cards, I don't know. But he promised to send the alarm."

"I hope you're right," said Russell, turning back toward the O'Learys'.

Russell's mother and father joined the crowd on De Koven, stoically helping douse the fire with pots they'd brought from home. Every nearby well and rain barrel was put to use, but hauling the water and carrying it to the flames was slow and awkward. Much water was splashed and lost. Two men hoisted a full barrel on their shoulders and dumped it on James Dalton's now smoking porch. Russell felt a surge of pride in these brave people. He passed yet another bucket of water to outstretched hands as the heat from the growing fire made the skin on his face singe.

Neighbors for an entire block past the O'Leary house were out of their homes now, most dragging everything of value into the streets in fear their own homes were next. Tables, chairs, mattresses, cooking utensils, all piled in the middle of the road, with children huddled among them. Some began to load wagons to escape if they had to, but Russell knew that many people in this area were too poor to own wagons or horses, and if they had to get away, it would be on foot.

"Where are the blasted engines?" shouted Patrick O'Leary. His own children were in the street with neighbors' children, and Catherine was slapping at the burning sidewalk with a wet towel. "It's been twenty minutes, they should be here!"

But they weren't. The fire, urged by the wind, blew across the backyards to Taylor Street, setting several rooftops ablaze. Some De Koven residents followed with their water buckets.

Russell knew the only hope was the fire engines, which, incredibly, had still not appeared on the scene. He shouted to his parents, "I'm going for the engines again!" and ran the three blocks to the drugstore. He slammed through the front door and found Bruno Goll inside, calmly counting money behind the counter. Russell shouted, "There's a fire on De Koven! Have you sent an alarm?"

Mr. Goll sniffed. "Why, yes, not long ago I did."

"Then give me the key," said Russell. "It did not get through. I will send another."

"No, I've seen an engine pass. I won't send another."

"Then the engine driver must be confused, because it hasn't come to De Koven!" Russell felt anger in his chest as hot as a fire.

"The alarm's sent!" insisted Mr. Goll. "Why are you accusing me? Now get out, I'm going to lock up to watch the fire myself!"

Russell wanted to grab the man up and shake him for the key, but of course the man was telling the truth. He had no reason to lie. Rushing out the door, he was met by a group of people heading toward De Koven to see the blaze. Russell hurried with them to the intersection of De Koven and Clinton Street, and drew up in shock.

The fire had spread drastically, with still no sign of the fire engines. The O'Learys were at the end of the block, staring back at the blaze that had totally consumed their home and those of their neighbors and was now burning the very ground on which the homes had stood as well as some of the furniture abandoned in the middle of the road. William Lee's family had found an empty lot on the south side of the street, and they sat in the dry grass, clinging to each other and to Patrick O'Leary's shivering calf.

"It happened so fast!" William called to Russell. He had his arm around his wife, who was crying quietly. Russell thought William's voice sounded as if he, too, was on the verge of tears. "If something isn't done soon it will be as bad as the one Saturday night!"

"No," said Russell. "That couldn't happen!"

"It could, Russell!"

Spectators rimmed the sidewalks of Clinton, pointing and staring as shanties, sheds, and trees went up in a progressively rapid succession just a half-block away. Russell pressed through the thick of them, trying to get ahead of the blaze. "Won't someone come with me?" he shouted to the crowd. "Folks up ahead are going to need warnings and help!"

One blond young man answered, "We're ready for an adventure, we'll come, won't we, Paddy?"

Paddy, a short boy with bristly hair, said, "I'll be a hero, you just wait!" And the two ran after Russell, cheering and laughing with each other as if they were off to the cockfights. Russell didn't slow down; if they meant to help they would keep up. The fire had set a dreadful pace, like a sprinter hell-bent on winning some sort of ghastly race, but he would give it a run for its money.

At last there was the sound of fire bells clanging and horses' hooves clattering over the noise of the fire and wind and shouts. Two engines passed on the street, one a hose cart that could only throw water short distances, and the other one an old, out-of-date steamer. They were headed for De Koven, but Russell knew they had a job ahead that would require five times as many engines.

Russell and the two young men crossed Taylor Street, dodging panicked goats, pigs, and people in the middle of the intersection. Overhead, the wind carried blazing debris like kites on the air. Russell felt sparks land on his neck. He batted them away and pushed ahead.

Three blocks ahead the fire was still only a threat, but most of the citizens were already in the road with their furniture and clothes, some in wagons with harnessed mules and horses, ready to flee. They stared at the approaching smoke and flames, yelling to each other, "Fire engines are on their way. They'll get it before it reaches us, God willing!" Several little girls, unalarmed because of their parents' stoic manner, played hopscotch in the road dust, giggling with each toss of the pebble.

One stooped, bearded man was in his yard behind a

wobbly fence, clutching a yellow kitten. Russell called over the fence, "Sir, we are here to help you empty your house and get out. There are only two fire engines fighting the blaze at the moment. We cannot take a chance! It is traveling much faster than you can imagine!"

The bearded man's eyes turned in Russell's direction, but his head did not move. "It don't dare come bother me," he said. "Fire come last winter and burned my house down good and flat. Built it up again with the help of my sons. It don't dare come after me again. I won't let it!"

"He's crazy!" one woman in the road shouted to Russell. "He won't listen to reason, never has!"

The blond man with Russell said to the old man, "I see you've got a hand cart there in the side yard."

"We'll help you pack," offered Paddy.

"No," said the old man. "Fire don't dare bother me!"

"Sir," Russell tried again. "I hope you're right. But it does no harm to be ready."

"He's a lunatic," called the woman in the road.

From down the block, there was the sound of more fire engines coming to the scene. *Four more, maybe five*, Russell estimated. *That's still not enough!* A man ran from behind a house on the south side of the road, waving his hands wildly and crying, "Get out, get out! I seen it, and it's the devil's work! Fire engines are pumping all they can, but the water boils away! Get out!"

As if to prove the man was right, there was suddenly

a burning shirt in the air, flying over rooftops from the direction of the blaze, its arms outstretched and flapping. It landed on a dead shrub in the old man's yard, and the shrub went up with a whoosh.

"Sweet Jesus!" cried one woman, and the rest of the residents joined in her screaming appeals. There was a scramble into wagons and a grabbing of reins and whips. Those without wagons hoisted their trunks onto shoulders and snatched up the bundles and boxes as best they could. As they rambled and pushed toward the end of the road, Russell heard, "Never thought it would come this far!" "God be with us!" "Hurry, May-belle, and don't drop that doll for we shan't come back to get her!"

Russell, Paddy, and the young blond man stood in the road, looking at the old man with his kitten as his shrub burned like tinder in a fireplace, and sparks fell to his grass and began to smolder.

"Come with us!" Russell called firmly. "We won't let you die here, sir."

"Yes," echoed Paddy. "We'll drag you out if we have to. Sir." Russell could hear the uncertainty in his voice and could feel the uncertainty in his own gut.

The old man stroked the kitten's fur, looking not at the three men in the road but at the golden night sky to the south. His long white beard blew around his face in the wind. "Been pushed around my whole life," he said. "Always been told what to do. My wife. Bosses down to the train yard. Last year, fire told me to get out of my house, it was gonna burn it down. But not anymore."

Russell knew the only thing to do would be to take the man by force. "May I hold your kitten?" he asked slowly.

The old man continued to stare at the sky, but he began to move backward toward his house.

"It's a nice cat," said Paddy. "May we hold it?"

"Don't tell me what to do," hissed the old man.

"We aren't," said Russell. "Sir, we only want to . . ."

The old man turned more quickly than Russell would have thought possible, ran inside, and slammed the door. Russell and the two men raced through the gate and beat on the door. It was locked tight.

"Curses!" said Paddy. "What do we do now?"

Another piece of flying, smoking debris landed in the yard by their feet. "I know what I'm doing," said the blond man. "Enough of this lark, I'm no hero. I've got to get back round to my own house on South Canal. You coming, Paddy?"

Paddy glanced at Russell, at the old man's house, and then at his friend, who shook his head, turned, and ran off. "In a minute. Let me give the codger one last chance to save himself."

"Thank you," said Russell.

"Don't thank me yet."

They kicked the door, but it didn't give. They went to the side of the house and smashed the window glass. There were curses from inside, and suddenly the kitten jumped through the shards and into the yard and clawed its way into the branches of a barren apple tree. "Sir!" called Russell. "Let us in!"

"Go away!" And then shutters inside the window

were slammed shut and locked. Russell went to the other side of the house where the only other window was located, but that set of inside shutters had been locked as well.

The grass in the old man's yard had broken into patches of fire, and from over the roofs on the south side of the road, the approaching flames were taller now, closer, with the smoke rolling across the road in the wind like a mist. Russell covered his nose and drove his fist into the glass and the wood of the shutter. He saw the cut on his knuckles but didn't feel it. "You're going to die, sir!"

"I've got an axe and I'll cut you to pieces if you don't leave me be!" came the cry from inside.

"Either he will kill us or the fire will!" shouted Paddy over the growing sound of the wind and oncoming blaze. "We have to get out of here!"

"Sir!" Russell screamed a last time, but the old man wouldn't answer. Paddy was right, and Russell felt sickened at the knowledge. He hurried to the apple tree, scooped up the trembling kitten, and buttoned it inside his shirt with the tiny yellow head peeking out. The kitten mewed and tried to scratch, but couldn't get out.

They made it to the end of the block and then down another, dodging a steam engine with its hoses and clanging bell and screaming drivers as it dashed down the middle of the street. The only thing Russell and Paddy could do was to get out of the way. The fire was winning its race.

They reached the tracks of the Galena and Chicago

Railroads next to the river off Harrison Street and stopped, bending over to catch their breath. At the moment they were out of harm's way. A cluster of frightened West Side citizens had also come to the tracks. They were coughing, crying, holding each other, and praying. A few had suitcases. Most, it seemed, had not had time to pack. One boy of about thirteen held tightly to a rope to which was tied a mangy, cream-colored dog. The dog saw the kitten and began to bark.

Russell rubbed the top of the kitten's head, trying to calm it down. He couldn't stop thinking about the old man locked in his house. His mind played and replayed an image of the flames crossing the road, engulfing the cottage. He could see the man cowering behind his bed, realizing that it was too late, that he was going to die. Russell dropped down onto the tracks, his head spinning. *God, bring a miracle to that poor old man, or let him perish quickly without pain and realization!* He could taste the soot in his mouth and smell the ash in his nostrils. Around him, the chatter was frightened but laced with a cautious hope.

"There's lots of fire engines out by now," came a young woman's voice. "They may stop the fire before it gets to my house. I live down on Ellsworth."

"The worst will be over soon," said a middle-aged man.

The talk went on and on, for a long time, becoming just a buzzing of noise in Russell's ears, none of it clear or intelligible.

But then Paddy shouted, "Look, it's shifted! It's

coming this way!" The crowd turned to stare, and they were frozen for a moment in horror.

"We've got to go back south," shouted another man, "or try to make the Van Buren Street Bridge."

"No!" said Paddy, pointing. "There are new flames there, too! We must cross the river here!"

There were shouts of "I can't swim! We're doomed!"

There were scattered beams and logs by the tracks, and Russell picked up a heavy beam and dragged it across to the edge of the river. The bank was steep, but not long. "You who can't swim," he said. "Take these in the water! Hold on for your lives, and you will survive! Don't be afraid!"

"But the babies?" said one mother with an infant in her arms and a toddler holding her hand.

"You need free hands for the boy," said Russell. "Put the baby in your blouse, like this cat! Don't be modest, there is no time!" The woman unbuttoned her blouse and slipped the baby inside, then buttoned it up again and tied it tightly closed with her shawl. The baby's eyes peeked out, wide and dark.

The people dragged the wood to the bank and slid down with it into the water. There were screams of fear and calls of encouragement all around. Paddy and Russell were the last to go, slipping along the weeds into the cold water, holding separate ends of a broken railroad tie. The kitten mewed, trying to free itself from Russell's shirt.

They paddled to the other side of the river behind the others on their floats, fighting the current with desperate arms and legs. A barge carrying grain nearly sideswiped them, but they kicked hard and made it past just in time. The boat crew saw all the people in the water and shouted for them to be careful.

On the eastern bank, Russell clawed his way to the top of the retaining wall with the others. He clasped Paddy's hand and said, "You're a good man, Paddy. God bless you. Now there is someone I have to find before it's too late. If the fire leaps the river, she's in danger, and I can't let that happen! I love her!"

He made his way to Market Street, which led north, and as soon as he caught his breath, began to run in his soggy coat, the frightened kitten bouncing and hissing.

# 16

Katina fought with her arms and legs, pushing against the water and the slime at the bottom of the river, holding her breath even as her lungs demanded she open her mouth and breathe. She could hear nothing but the hissing of her own blood in her ears. *I can't escape a fire only to drown in this hellish river!*

One foot found a solid spot on the bottom, and with all her strength, she pushed with it and felt herself moving upward. Her arms battled the water, her teeth were clenched to keep from drawing in water. Her skirt tangled around her, but she spun, throwing it loose. Her lungs burned, telling her to breathe, *breathe!*

And then her head broke the surface and she gasped. Fresh air flooded her lungs, making her feel faint. *I made it! Yes!* But then the weight of her clothes pulled at her again, and she began to sink. "No!" she screamed as her head was sucked under. Her arms fought, but did not hold her up. The world was drawn upward and away again.

Her thrashing hand struck something hard and cylindrical, and instinctively she grabbed it. She clung as tightly as she could, needing again to have a breath, aching to have a breath, fighting to crawl up, but she couldn't, her skirt was wrapped around again and wouldn't shake free.

*I have to breathe!*

The thing she was clutching began to move upward, dragging her with it. Again her head broke the surface, and she gulped the air. Her eyes were filmy and she could see only hazy lights around her, but she could hear voices nearby.

"Grab her arms! Get her out, before she's gone!"

Katina was hoisted up and onto a solid surface, where she lay panting and rubbing her eyes to see.

"Miss, are you all right?" came a deep voice.

Katina's voice was raspy and faint. "I don't know. Where am I? Who are you?"

"Martin Moberg, crew of the *Lady L*," said the voice. "Heading out to the lake before we catch on fire! Saw you strike the water before our very eyes, knocked off the bridge you were, and we fished you out with a pole."

Katina forced herself to sit up. Beside her were two sailors, and all around the deck were barrels and bundles. Her head rolled, and she put her hand to her eyes. "We're going out to the lake?"

"Best place for now! The fire's just jumped the river south of here. The wind is fierce, with no sign of letting up. The lake will be safest."

"Safest," said Katina. She bent over and coughed. "Yes, safest . . . That is best . . ."

"Don't know how far the blaze will go," said the sailor. He was young and handsome, with wind-chapped skin. He wore a white hat with a black band. "But we ain't waitin' round to see. It's going to be every man for himself tonight!"

*Every man for himself.* Katina rubbed her eyes and they at last came into focus. The boat was moving ahead steadily, with the Madison Street Bridge behind them and the Randolph Street Bridge straight ahead. Just past that the river turned sharply to the right and, joined with the water from the North Branch, flowed through the main part of the city and into Lake Michigan. *Every man for . . .*

"No, let me off, please!" she said. "There are people I care about, I can't leave them alone!"

The sailor laughed in disbelief. "Miss, do you hear yourself? What can you do against the fire?"

"I can do what I can do!"

"Miss?"

Katina got to her feet. They were moving under the Randolph Street Bridge. Spectators lined that bridge as they had the Madison Street Bridge.

Katina's head was aching and her ears were still humming from the fall into the water, but her voice was strong. "Let me off this boat!"

"We can't!"

The boat emerged from beneath the bridge and was steered toward the wider mouth of the Chicago River. As it took the turn, it came close to the log-reinforced wall on the riverbank, and Katina pulled herself up onto several bundles and stood, the wind whipping her face. Her soaked skirt hugged her legs. The wall was at least five feet from the boat. *Can I make it?*

"No!" cried Martin. The sailor came up behind her and reached for her arm just as she dove off the boat, her hands outstretched. She slammed into the wall and slid downward, but her shoes dug as hard as they could into the wood, and her fingers clutched the splintery surface. She stopped sliding and began climbing upward. Behind her she could hear the sailor shout, "Good luck, little lady! You're a mad one at that, but good luck!"

*Godspeed, Martin Moberg!*

Summoning all her strength, Katina pulled herself to the top of the wall. Her wet clothes were heavy, and the muscles of her right leg locked into a cramp. She muffled a cry and forced herself up and over, where she rolled to her side and drew her leg up to massage the painful knot.

She squinted at the sky. There were still stars visible amid thin ribbons of smoke. She couldn't cross the river to find Russell, so she would go back to Homeplace. *No, Homeplace is destroyed, burned to ashes last night by John Brandermill.* She would return to the Stick. The fire would be stopped, certainly, before it got that far. She would wait for Russell there. He would know to look for her at the Stick.

*If he is alive,* she thought.

"He is, and don't ever say that again!" she scolded

herself. With that, she pushed herself to her feet against the pain in her leg.

She was in the yard of a single-story warehouse with boarded-up windows, surrounded on three sides by a tall, solid plank fence. Her heart pounded in her ears, and the sound of the fire alarm bells made her feel unsteady on her feet. *I'm going to faint,* she thought. *I've never fainted before. I wonder what it feels like . . .*

But something deeper inside her mind said, *Katina! Don't you dare give in now! Get out of this place!*

With that, she went about finding a way out of the warehouse yard. The gate was locked. There were barrels and crates by the short wharf on the riverside, but the barrels were too heavy to push over to roll, and the crates too big to lift. So she crouched down and began to push. With her jaw set and her shoulders tight, she pushed and huffed until the first of the crates had furrowed a path across the warehouse yard to the fence. It would take another two to make a step tall enough to climb over. She pushed a second crate over, but could not lift it on top of the first. She dug her fingers under the edge and screamed with the effort, but neither will nor noise made it go up more than several inches before dropping back to the ground.

She stomped her good foot. "I've got to get out!"

One of the warehouse windows had been poorly boarded, with a good seven inches of glass showing at the bottom. Katina lifted her skirt, wrapped her hand, and smashed in the glass. She shook the shards from her skirt, then pulled herself up to stand on the sill. Once she'd gained her balance, she climbed onto the shingled roof. Standing precariously on the sloped surface, she edged around to the other side of the building, where the fence was close enough to straddle. On the other side of the fence was a straw-lined wagon which likely was used to carry crates of fragile items to the warehouse. The wagon was empty except for the straw, and Katina was thankful for the bit of luck. She eased her legs over the side of the fence and dropped into the straw. A new firebrand of pain shot up through the cramped muscle of her leg, but she sat still for a moment, massaging the knot, and then she got out of the wagon and into the street.

On the river side of Market Street were huge wooden grain elevators, warehouses, smokestacked factories, and office buildings. Businesses, hotels, and nicer apartments, also made of wood, lined the other side. Tonight the street was buzzing with people who, having been awakened by the increasingly insistent fire alarms, swarmed toward the bridges to see the blaze. Katina watched them as she stood holding on to the wagon and catching her breath. She realized suddenly how tired she was, and wondered if she had the strength to make it back to Quincy Street.

*I have to get back there*, she told herself, biting her lip to keep the tears from coming. Several carriages rattled by, and she could see the occupants staring out the windows for a glimpse of the fire. If only they would offer her a ride. But of course they would not.

She began to walk, counting her steps to take her mind off her weakness. *I can't give in to this*, she insisted to her shaking body. *I'm strong. I can make it.*

She stayed out of the way of the curious crowd, clinging to the sides of the buildings and rubbing her eyes to keep the world in focus. Above the tall hotels and banks, she could see the sky growing brighter, obscuring the stars, as if the sun were rising in the southwest. She crossed the intersection of Washington Street, and then Madison, where half a block to the right the two crowds—those crossing the bridge from the west and those still coming to have a look—ran head-on into each other. She counted her breaths as well as her steps now. Her mouth tasted of bile and the river water she had swallowed.

*Three more blocks,* she thought. *I'll get there.*

She could see that the flames were close, perhaps one block south of Quincy now, having been blown up the east side of the river.

*God help us!*

At the corner of Quincy and Market Street, there was nothing but bedlam. People who had been caught unaware, sleeping in their flats, were making a scramble to save some of their possessions before the wall of fire leaped into their street. There was a rain of sheets, pillows, coats, and books showering down to the road from second-, third-, and fourth-floor windows. Some people were already evacuating; others stood in the street, clutching what they could, crying out for family members who were not visible in the crowd. Thieves from Conley's Patch were helping themselves to items left unattended on the street, scooping up all they could hold and laughing. An old woman's soup cart had overturned in front of a wagon, and the wagon passengers were screaming at the old woman. The horse at harness was snorting, the old woman was crying, the passengers were chastising her, and all Katina could think was, *She didn't mean it. It wasn't her fault, it was out of her control. Leave her alone!*

*She didn't mean it!*

The smoke was thick. Overhead, flaming shingles arced above the rooftops and landed on the sidewalk at Katina's feet.

The fire was here.

There was nothing to stop it now. Katina felt as if the earth beneath her feet had begun to shake. Like a mountain crumbling into the sea.

Like a Georgian mansion giving up its ghost to the torches of maniacal renegades.

*I didn't mean it. Mother, Katherine, it wasn't my fault, I didn't mean it. Russell, I didn't mean it!*

And then the earth buckled one last time, and Katina dropped to the road in a dead faint.

# 17

*❦*

Russell had reached Quincy Street well ahead of the fire and had gone directly to the Stick to find Katina. He was soaked to the skin and covered with soot, but the way he looked meant nothing. Finding her meant everything.

*I cannot wait to hold her,* he'd thought. *To touch her hair and tell her how much I love her.*

But Alice had met him inside the Stick, where customers who had grown bored with the fire across the river had come to resume their drinking, cigar smoking, and merrymaking. She told him that she had no idea where Katina was, but the expression on her face told Russell something was wrong.

Russell wriggled the kitten out from his shirt and put it on the floor, where it staggered, shook itself off, and began to prowl the shadows beneath a nearby table and bat at dust balls. Alice said, "How precious! Did you save that little thing?"

But Russell took her by the shoulder and looked sternly into her eyes. "Are you sure you don't know where Katina is? She might be in her attic room, away from the noise."

"She isn't there, I know it," said Alice. The girl's lips rolled in between her teeth nervously. "She went with me out to the bridge to watch the fire, but she didn't come back. She said she wanted to cross over to the West Side."

"Why would she do that?"

"She wanted to go look for you. She knew your parents lived on De Koven."

"What!"

"She said she had to find you, no matter what."

Russell's heart sank. He shook his head, as if denying it would make it untrue. "That's impossible!"

"It's true, but maybe she's all right," offered Alice hesitantly. "She's smart, smarter than me, for sure. She ain't gonna run smack into a fire. You know how scared she is of fire."

Russell let go of Alice and went to the open door to stare out at the citizens of Quincy Street who had taken up vigil in the road, no longer staring at the inferno from the riverside but now waiting to see if their own homes and shops would be in peril. A few had brought out some bundles, but most were empty-handed. Ladies were huddled together, speaking to one another with grim faces; men were cross-armed and frowning, glancing around and at the sky. An old soup-seller had found an opportunity and was wheeling her cart among the people, offering cups of steaming pepper soup for three pennies a serving.

Someone touched Russell's arm. It was Madame Jocelyn, holding a cup of hot tea. "You look a fright, son," she said. "Like somebody dipped you in oil and rolled you in black flour."

Russell took the cup of tea, but his hand shook so hard he couldn't drink it. He put the cup down on the corner of a table. "I have to find her," he said.

Madame Jocelyn pointed her wrinkled finger at his face. "Now you talkin' stupid, mister. How many thousands of people in Chicago? How many thousands on the West Side? And in the middle of the biggest fire we ever seen? Sit down, have something stronger than that blasted tea, and ease your worries. Alice, get us a couple brandies."

"Ma'am," said Russell. "You know I am not one to give up, ever, when something is important."

Madame Jocelyn's nose twitched. "And you're a lunatic! You won't make it back 'cross that river now, not for the love of God or money. And if you did, you'd be burned up in your tracks. What good is that?"

At the piano, the tune changed from a light, plinky ditty to a slow and somber hymn. One drunk at the bar turned on his seat, raised his glass, and said, "This is for them poor unfortunates on the other side of the river what is burned up in hell's fire! May God keep their souls safe, and keep us safe from that same fire!"

"Here, here!" said another man.

"To the dead and the living," said the girl at the piano. There was a second of silence as everyone in the saloon took a long swig from their glasses, jars, and bottles, then the laughter and shouts began again.

*Katina*, Russell thought, his fingers taking hold of the door frame and squeezing so hard that splinters were driven into his skin. *Please, wherever you are, be alive!*

Alice brought two glasses half-filled with dark liquid, and Madame Jocelyn took one while Alice held the tray with the other toward Russell. He looked at it and said, "No, thank you."

"C'mon, you old starched-britches," said Madame Jocelyn with an attempt at a smile. "It'll take the sting off o' life. You'll feel better."

Russell's arm shot out and knocked the glass from the tray. "I don't want to feel better!" he shouted. "I want to find Katina!"

With that, he darted out to the street and into the milling mob.

A fire engine raced past on Quincy and then turned south on Fifth Avenue, spraying rocks and dirt from the dry road surface. People jumped out of the way. Beside and behind the smoking contraption ran more firefighters, their faces tight with determination, their arms swinging in militaristic unison.

"Fire's but two blocks away!" cried one fireman through his horn. "Be prepared!"

The crowd began shifting nervously, looking up at the air. The smoke was growing thicker, darker. Several large smoldering chunks of debris drifted from over the buildings and down to the street at their feet.

It was then that the people saw the truth. Their street was going to burn, and soon.

While Russell stamped on the flaming chunks that had struck the road, other folks scattered like dust in the wind, making for their shacks, their tenements, their apartments, and their gambling halls and shops, to collect what they could. Another fire engine rattled past, and Russell knew he had to make a decision.

*I must stay here and help these people get out,* he thought. *Or I can look for Katina.* The choice cut his heart like a razor. How could he choose? It was as if he were being asked which leg he would prefer to have amputated, his right or his left.

Across the street, upstairs tenement windows were slammed open, and people began throwing things down to the road. Buckets, blankets, dolls, baskets, tools. Anything that wouldn't break came tumbling down, and some things that did. More embers and ash blew overhead and landed on Quincy Street rooftops, none of them large enough to set the roofs on fire, but a foreshadowing of what was to come. People who had been sleeping through the ordeal were now awakening, gazing from their windows and rubbing their eyes, then screaming at the realization of what was happening.

Family wagons, driven by fathers or sons and hitched to horses from nearby stables, pulled up in front of the tenements on both sides of the street and braked. Horses danced nervously in place as families threw their crates, mattresses, and other bundles into the wagons, then scooped up from the road the items they'd thrown down. Bandits emerged from the dark underground rooms of Conley's Patch and took advantage of the confusion to steal what they could.

With dismay, Russell saw Bruce Charles darting back and forth, stuffing his pockets full of forks and spoons and odd, broken trinkets from the road dust.

"Bruce!" he shouted at the boy. He ran over and grabbed Bruce by the arm, then turned the boy's coat pockets inside out, dumping out the contents. "What are you doing? You're stealing!"

Bruce yanked his arm away from Russell, his face contorted with shame and denial. "But they don't need these! It's only spoons and such! They'd be stamped to bits in the road!"

"It's wrong to steal!"

"I'm not stealing! I'm helping myself!"

"Will you never learn?" Russell shouted. "Will nothing ever change? I've accomplished nothing, I've wasted my time!"

Bruce spun away.

"Bruce, come back!"

But the boy was gone, vanished in the crowd.

*This is my answer!* he thought, heartsick. *What I've done here has been a waste of time. But I will find Katina! God, let her be alive, and if not, let me die in my efforts, for living would be unbearable.*

He forced his way against the crowd, imagining the difficulty he would find trying to cross the bridge. But he would fight if he had to in order to get through. He would go all the way back to De Koven, every fiery step of the way.

There was an old woman crying in the middle of the road. It was the soup-seller. The terrified woman had her hands cupped over her ears. *I can't stop for her, I haven't time!* Russell thought, but he knew he had to, if only for a moment.

"Ma'am, where do you live?" he asked. "The fire is coming and you can't stay here!"

She whispered, "I don't have a home."

"Where do you sleep?"

"In the tunnels beneath Billy Spilman's dance hall. I cook in the alley."

"Have you anything you want from beneath the dance hall?" he pressed. "You'll need to get north quickly!"

"I have nothing but my clothes on my back and this cart, and 'tis stuck in a deep rut in this bloody road!"

"Then let me help you move your cart. It is your livelihood, and you won't want to lose it."

But before Russell could rock the cart wheel out of the hole, a wagon bearing a family and its belongings came barreling down Quincy, straight at them. Russell leaped out of the way, dragging the old woman with him, as the horse pulling the wagon whinnied and tried to jump the soup cart. Its hind legs came down on the cart, smashing it to bits, and the front right wheel of the wagon struck the cart and shattered.

The man in the wagon jumped out of the wagon and threw his hands in the air. The woman in the wagon pointed a threatening finger at the old woman and cursed her at the top of her lungs. "Look what you've done, you witch!" The children in the wagon began to cry.

Russell took hold of the horse's reins and walked it forward, freeing its legs from the wreckage. The man yelled at Russell, at the old woman, at his wife.

"We're doomed with a broken wheel!" he wailed. "We're destroyed! How will we escape now?"

Several flaming cinders fell to the road beside Russell and the horse. There was little time to argue.

"You'll have to carry what you can!" Russell said. "The children can ride the horse, and you lead."

The man continued to complain, the old woman and the children continued to cry, and Russell thought, *This delay may cost me Katina! Why did I even bother to stop?*

And then he saw her, ten feet past the wreck, staring straight ahead as if in a trance. Her clothes were soaked, her body quivering. He blinked, certain he was dreaming.

But he was not.

*Katina!*

Her eyes rolled up in her head and she dropped to the road amid the pounding of feet and hooves and wagon wheels.

# 18

Russell carried Katina inside the Stick, where some of the patrons were still at the bar, drinking their glasses of whiskey, and others were at tables, dealing out cards. Madame Jocelyn was on a chair at a corner table, calmly puffing on a pipe and dangling a string for the little yellow kitten to catch. Alice was pacing back and forth near the door, and she gasped when Russell came in and lay Katina on the bar.

"You've found her!" Alice cried. "And she's dead!"

"No," said Russell. "She is alive, only overcome. I need to revive her, and then we all need to get out of here immediately. The rooftops across the street are beginning to smolder!"

Alice patted Katina's face tentatively, but Russell pushed her aside and began to shake Katina firmly. "Katina!" he called. "You must wake up!" And to Madame Jocelyn, "Ma'am! You have to evacuate right now! There is no hope that anything will be spared, and the fire is breathing down our necks like the hounds of hell!"

But the old woman only took her pipe out from between her teeth and said, "It won't burn the Stick. Nothing dares to confront me. You know my reputation."

"Stubbornness won't keep the flames away!" Russell said. "An old man perished in his cottage today for worthless contempt! Do what I say! Alice, there is but a moment. If there is anything you need, get it now or never!"

Most of the men, drunk as they were, seemed to catch Russell's urgency. They wrapped their arms about each other's shoulders and stumbled for the door. Only three at the gambling table waved Russell off with a flick of their hands, and one wobbly patron said, "Got a bet going here. If I win, the wind's gonna shift and go back where it came!" His gambling partners howled with laughter.

Alice ran up the steps behind the piano. Madame Jocelyn continued to smoke her pipe and play with the kitten.

"Katina," said Russell, fanning his hand. "Wake up, I have no wagon to put you in, and we'd do so much better if you were awake!"

Katina groaned slightly.

"Wake up!"

Slowly, Katina's eyes opened, unfocused at first, then steadying and locking squarely on Russell's face.

"Oh," she managed. "Russell, is it you?"

Russell nodded.

"Truly?"

"Yes," Russell said. "We've got to be moving."

"The fire, dear! Did you see the fire coming?"

"Yes, but we will get out. It is catching across the street. Can you walk?"

Holding Katina around her waist, Russell lifted her to her feet. She grimaced as if her leg hurt, but said nothing. "I can walk," she said. "Russell, I can't believe you are here. I will wake up any moment and be back in the warehouse yard!"

"You are soaked!"

"And so are you."

"I've been in the river," said Russell.

"And so have I!" said Katina.

"I hated being in the river!"

"So did I," she said, smiling at last. The smile was the most beautiful thing Russell had seen in his lifetime. Then her smile vanished, and tears came into her eyes. She said, "I'm sorry, Russell. I didn't trust you and I should have."

"I wasn't understanding, I wasn't patient," said Russell. He held Katina's face in his hands, then kissed her fully. "I was coming to find you," he said. "I resented an old woman and her cart stuck in the road for slowing me down. But if it wasn't for that, I would not have stopped, and I would not have seen you."

"Things happen for a reason," said Katina hoarsely. "It's destiny."

"I love you," said Russell. "And we have to go!"

Several dresses were tossed down the steps, and then a brocade satchel, which landed squarely on the piano keys with a plunk. Then Alice could be heard up the stairs, "Becky is up here! And I can't get her out, she's too sick, she's too heavy!"

Through the open front door came a billow of smoke. Russell glanced outside. The tenement directly across the street had caught fire; the roof was blazing. Some of the upstairs windows belched flames, and in other upstairs windows, tenants screamed that the stairs were on fire and there was no way down.

"We must get Becky!" cried Katina.

This broke Madame Jocelyn's spell. She dropped her pipe to the tabletop and scooped up the kitten, who uttered a startled meow. She snatched Katina's satchel from the piano keys, put the kitten inside, and buckled it up. "Let's go, boys!" she said to the gamblers, but the men at the card table glowered and sat tight, holding their cards, as if daring anyone to make them move.

Russell darted for the steps, and Katina tried to follow, but still seemed weak, for she grabbed onto the edge of a table and stopped, leaning over. "Get outside with Madame Jocelyn," Russell shouted. "And go into Rat's Alley. Alice and I will get Becky and meet you there!"

"But Russell—" began Katina, but Madame Jocelyn took her arm and said, "He's right, girl. We got to move!"

They hurried out the door, Katina's satchel on Madame Jocelyn's right elbow, Katina on her left.

Russell raced up the steps to the second floor. Alice was inside the third bedroom, standing beside Becky's simple iron bed, one hand over her mouth, staring at the window. The glass had been broken from flying debris, and the windowsill had caught fire. "We're going up!" Alice shrieked. "The Stick's burning!"

Becky was sitting up in bed, teetering back and forth. Her red hair was loose and stringy, hanging down her nightgown. "I'm sick," she said simply. "I can't run."

"Just hold on to us," said Alice. She bent down and Becky grasped her neck. Russell slid his arm around Becky's waist. She was hot with fever, and moving her was going to be difficult.

*But we have to try!*

The curtains in the window went up in a flash, and fire reached around to the wall, igniting the dirty flowered wallpaper with a crackle and pop.

Holding Becky as tightly as they could, they walked her out the door and eased her down the steps. Russell knew things were going from bad to worse when he saw the smoke in the stairwell, rolling up from the first floor. Then came the shouts of the cardplayers, and Alice cried out, "Fire's downstairs, too! We're done for!"

The scene at the bottom of the staircase confirmed their worst fears. Fire had blown across the street and had set the left side of the door frame ablaze, and cinders had landed inside on one of the threadbare rugs, making it burst into flame. The table nearest the door was burning, as was part of the dry pine floor beneath it.

The gamblers were gaping, at last having dropped their cards in a flutter. One held his bowler hat to his chest as if out of respect for the fire. "I've died and gone to hell," he said, his voice slurring. "Looka this, Morgan, we gonna meet the devil together!"

"Bring 'em on, the butcher! Always meant to face him head-on!" said another.

"Meet him later!" said Russell. "Give yourself another day to bet, another day for drinking."

"Good point!" said the gambler with the bowler hat. He picked up an open decanter of whiskey and cradled it in his arm.

Alice, Russell, and the three gamblers, with Becky between them, made their way to the door. The gamblers went out first. Alice and Russell carried Becky out next. The stoop was burning, so they had to jump from the door to the ground. Russell's face and arms were struck with nearly intolerable heat. He could barely believe what he was seeing. The flames across the street were at least a hundred feet tall, clawing at the sky like talons. Wagons left unattended along the road were ablaze, as were crates and bundles left behind by those who had escaped. People still ran in the street, confused and terrified, attempting to carry whatever of value they could handle, stumbling, dodging the fiery rain. A fire engine, hooked into the hydrant near the corner, had its canvas hose and powerful stream of water aimed at the tenement directly across from the Stick. The tenement was engulfed but was not empty, and a thin mattress was being pushed out of a fourth floor window by a hysterical mother. Tucked beneath the sheets around the mattress were two little children, their faces barely visible.

"They're going to fall!" shouted Alice.

And they did indeed fall, straight to the ground with a *thunk*. There was no cry, no scream. Russell was certain the children were dead. The mother swung her legs out of the window, where red tongues of fire were lapping out after her, and she paused only a second before letting go and plummeting to the street. She struck and collapsed in a heap, silent, motionless.

"This isn't happening!" screamed Alice.

Embers filled the air, raining down upon them. Russell and Alice hauled Becky between them, heading north for Rat's Alley, with the gamblers close behind, cursing each time a cinder landed on their heads, the one with the whiskey decanter cradling it as if it were a baby. *By now, Rat's Alley might be in flames*, Russell thought. But the alley cut to Adams, and then another alley cut over to Monroe and then Madison.

*If we stay this course we will end up on Franklin Street*, Russell thought, *and then it will just be a short distance to a bridge across the Chicago River to North Division, where, God willing, the fire will not follow!*

They reached the entrance to Rat's Alley and turned in to it as the roof of the rattletrap bakery on the corner blew off in flaming chunks. Russell was struck on the back with a shingle. It sizzled through his shirt to the flesh, but he shook it off, gritted his teeth, and held on to Becky. One of the gamblers was struck in the leg by a shingle that set his trouser leg on fire, but he tore the trousers off, threw them aside, and caught up to the others in his long johns.

Then Alice screamed, "Becky's on fire!"

Becky, who had tried her best to keep her feet moving between Russell and Alice, was so dazed that she was unaware that an ember had landed in the back of her hair and set it afire.

Alice let go of Becky's arm and slapped her friend's hair with her hands. The fire spread upward toward Becky's scalp. Alice screamed. Russell reached down for a handful of road dirt to throw at the girl.

But Becky realized at that moment what was happening, and she took off at a mad run. At the same time, the gambler with the decanter pitched the whiskey onto her, and her head and shoulders went up in a fireball.

"I meant to put it out!" the gambler wailed.

Becky's scream turned into a demon's shriek, and she covered her head with her hands, setting the sleeves of her nightgown on fire. Russell ran after her, threw her to the ground and rolled her over and over. He could see the girl's eyes, open, conscious, staring out through the flame. But her mouth was blistering, and all she could do was whimper.

Alice put her hands over her ears.

The gambler cried, "I din' mean it, I meant to put it out!"

But it was too late. Becky shuddered, then went limp, her gown still smoking, her entire face charred beyond recognition. Alice turned away and screamed. The gamblers stared. Russell whispered, "I do not understand. Let me understand these terrible things!" He said a quick prayer over the body, and Alice whispered, "Amen."

They left Becky in the road, for there was no more they could do for her.

They found Madame Jocelyn and Katina in the ruins of the old garment factory. Several buildings this far down the alley had roofs on fire, but none were yet engulfed. Trash and broken dishes littered the narrow, dusty stretch, and people were still dragging belongings out from the tenements. Russell wondered if some were hiding in the tunnels beneath the buildings, hoping the fire would go over them.

When Katina saw Russell, she fell into his arms. "Thank you!" she said, her breath soft on his neck, soothing the burns there. "Thank you for coming and finding us. With you, I know we'll be safe!"

Russell kissed her cheek and her hair, but he could not speak of Becky. Some things were too terrible on the tongue. Alice and the gamblers said nothing either, but it was only moments before Madame Jocelyn asked, "And where is our Miss Becky?"

Alice shook her head. It was enough.

Madame Jocelyn made a hardened sound in her throat, and Katina said, "God rest her soul!"

It was all they could offer in her memory, because the fire behind them was not slowing down, and the sound of sirens continued to grow louder in the night.

# 19

"We'll make it to the river," Russell said as they stepped from the ruins of the factory and into the alley. Katina opened her satchel to make sure the kitten was still safe. Its yellow head peeked out and it hissed, angry at its confinement. She closed the satchel back up. The three gamblers stared at the blazing buildings at the entrance to the alley. Madame Jocelyn, who somewhere along the way had lost a shoe, gazed at her bare toes as if she'd never seen them before.

"This fire will be under control before it gets to North Division," Russell continued. "Why, those rich folks over there wouldn't stand for it!" Katina tried to smile, knowing how hard he was trying. Her leg still ached, but not as badly. "But I need to stop at an abandoned house in the alley off Adams. Bruce lives underneath. If he's there—I pray God he is—I want him to come with us."

Katina leaned her head on Russell's shoulder. Even in all this tragedy, he felt so steady and secure.

The scraggly crew hurried down the alley, passing Brandermill's Boardinghouse. Katina glanced over at it, remembering her old life. *So long ago, it seemed. So very . . .*

The boardinghouse door slammed open, and two men came out. One was thin and clean-shaven. The other was older, with a bristly beard and thick brows.

*John Brandermill!*

"Well!" cried John Brandermill from the boardinghouse steps. "Look who we run into during the fire, Ardie! If it isn't the man who turned me in for killing Meg!"

"No!" said Katina.

Russell said nothing, but continued walking. Suddenly there was a gunshot, and a bullet bit the ground in front of Russell's feet. The group flinched and whirled around. Both men were pointing pistols at Russell. One was smoking. "I know it's you," said John. "Look like what they said, and you's with these people they say you spend time with. Them wenches, that short little gal. I thought I'd burned you up, but you're a tough old hide, ain't you?"

John and Ardie came down the steps, the guns still trained on Russell. "Gonna kill you, know that?" John grinned darkly.

"Let these others go," Russell said. The calm in his voice surprised Katina.

"Sure," said John. "The rest of you is free to leave."

The gamblers took the cue to heart. They were off

in a spray of dirt. But Madame Jocelyn, Alice, and Katina stood their ground.

*This isn't happening!* Katina thought.

The men with the pistols stopped just four feet in front of Russell. John shook his head and grinned. "My building's gonna burn in a few minutes. Everybody's gone, though, I closed the boardinghouse when I got outta jail. Didn't want to see their pitiful faces anymore, lookin' at me like I killed my wife. Been livin' alone in there, and I like it!"

"Leave your guns," said Russell. "Come with us and save yourselves."

"Ha!" said John. His beard twitched. "I don't think so. I said I like livin' alone. No tenants, no wife. Nice. Quiet. I like it." He sniffed. "But I don't like you, Russell Cosgrove."

"You don't have to like me," Russell began. "Just—"

The pistol went off again. The bullet whizzed by Russell's ear. Katina screamed and grabbed Russell's arm. Ardie laughed.

"Flame or gunshot?" asked John. "Which way you wanna die, Mr. Cosgrove? Lock you up in one of my closets and let the fire take you, or I can shoot you here. What'll it be?"

"Leave him alone!" demanded Katina.

"Want to die with him, lady?" asked Ardie.

"Katina," said Russell, pulling her hand from his arm and pushing her away. "It'll be all right."

"No, it won't!" she cried.

"Mr. Cosgrove, convince these ladies to go on, or I'll shoot them first," John said.

"Katina, please go," said Russell gently. And he gave Katina a wink that said, *I'll be all right, I have a plan. Just go and I'll catch up with you!*

Her heart twisting with fear, Katina began to back up, away from Russell and the men with the pistols. Beside her, Alice whispered, "Help him, Lord!"

Russell faced John. "Fight me without the pistol, John. Like two men."

"My pistol does my talking for me," John replied.

"I'll fight him, John!" said Ardie. "I'd like to kill him with my bare hands, like I killed my brother! Snap! Broken neck!"

John seemed to consider this. Katina continued to back up, stumbling over a broken chair left in the alley.

"We may all die in the fire, anyway," Russell pointed out matter-of-factly. "Might as well make a little sport out of it, a little wager?"

"A wager?" asked John. "What kind of wager?"

"You're a gambling man," said Russell. "If I win at fisticuffs with Ardie here, without so much as a scratch on myself, then you let me go. If Ardie is able to cut me, much less break my neck, then I've lost, and you can shoot me, lock me in a closet, your choice. Your win."

*This can't be happening,* Katina. thought frantically. *This is wrong. Let this be a dream, just a terrible dream!* All around them the roar of the fire grew louder, the smell of death and ash stronger and more bitter.

"Let me fight him, John!" yelled Ardie.

John looked dubious, then said, "Why not? I love a bet! But if you lose, I just might kill your women, too!"

Russell didn't respond to this. With his fists raised, he began skipping backward, toward the entrance to the alley where the buildings on both sides were engulfed in flames. Ardie threw down his pistol and went after him, swinging his fists in the air and snorting.

"I'm a good fighter! I'll knock you on your face, you coward!"

Russell took a quick step toward Ardie, threw a jab, then jumped back. He continued to move toward the alley entrance. John Brandermill followed at a close distance, pointing his gun at Russell and chuckling.

*Russell's getting John's attention away from us*, Katina thought. *He's giving us a chance to escape.*

Suddenly Ardie lunged at Russell and grabbed him around the waist, and they struck the graveled ground in the alley with an "ugh!" They rolled back and forth, Ardie trying to smash Russell's face, but Russell managing to lean his head away in time. Then Russell broke free, leaped to his feet, and ran to the corner of Quincy and the alley. He stood out amid the burning bits of roof and between the flaming shops. "Come and get me, Ardie!"

Ardie charged, bellowing, and Russell jumped out of the way in time to send Ardie sprawling. This gave Russell time to pick up the weapon he'd been after, a burning beam from the baker's roof. He gripped the unscorched end and swung the flaming end at Ardie's head. He caught the man in the jaw, and with a croak Ardie fell to the ground and did not move.

"I won!" shouted Russell above the din of the fire.

He held out his hands for John to see. "Not a cut on me!"

"Ardie's not dead," John yelled.

"I didn't say I'd kill him, just beat him."

"Get up, Ardie!" cried John. "Don't lose my bet!"

Ardie groaned but didn't get up.

*Thank God!* thought Katina, her heart rising. *Russell won the bet!*

John pointed his pistol at Russell. "Kill him or I'll kill you!"

There was the barest moment of hesitation. Then Russell shouted, "No!"

"Do it!"

"No."

*Russell!* Katina clutched Madame Jocelyn's arm. *Do what he says!*

But suddenly, with a deafening, splintering crack, the burning bakery gave way, the remainder of its roof falling in on itself, the heavy outer wall falling with a roar and a fiery crash of beams onto the road on top of Russell. He was gone, vanished beneath the inferno.

*"Noooo!"* Katina screamed. She leaped forward, but Madame Jocelyn caught her arm and held her back.

"Ha!" shouted John Brandermill. He began to dance in the road like a man at his wedding. "Fire did it for me! He's dead, burned up and gone!" John turned and called to the women, "Lost his bet, he did! Ha ha!" Then the man ran off up the alley, shouting and laughing.

Katina fell against Madame Jocelyn. "No, God, not this, tell me Russell's alive!"

"Shhh, he's gone," whispered Madame Jocelyn. "But we have to go on! There's nothing for us here anymore!"

"God, no!"

Alice wept soundlessly, holding Katina's hand. Katina's head spun in sickening swirls.

"We have to go to the river," said Madame Jocelyn.

"But—"

"No buts. Ain't no way back, the alley's blocked with the fire now. And he's gone, honey. Listen to me! Listen! It ain't safe to stay here. Russell would want us to save ourselves."

She couldn't feel her feet beneath her as she walked north, out of Rat's Alley, across Adams, and into the alley on the other side. Madame Jocelyn was talking to her, the woman's red-painted mouth was moving, but Katina couldn't hear her words.

*He's dead! There is nothing worth anything, nothing worth living for! Why, God? Is this destiny?*

They passed an empty two-story house with broken windows and a dilapidated porch, the only one in the alley, and a voice in Katina's mind said, *Stop.*

She stopped.

"What is it?" asked Alice.

This was the place Russell had described as Bruce's hideout. He had wanted to see if the boy was there.

*I can do what I can do.*

Russell had said that many times.

"I can do what I can do," whispered Katina.

"What?" asked Madame Jocelyn, tugging Katina's sleeve. "Missy, we have to keep on going!"

"I must look here," Katina said.

"Why?"

"It will take only a moment." Kneeling down, she peered into the empty, cobwebby space. "This is where Bruce lives. He might be here, hiding. Bruce? Are you there?"

There was silence. Madame Jocelyn stomped her bare foot impatiently.

"Bruce, it's Katina. If you are there, come with us! We're going to safety in North Division!"

A rat scuttled over her hands. She flinched but did not pull away. "Bruce?"

And then a small voice from deep in the black shadows, "I can't come with you."

"Why not?"

"I wasn't gonna do more bad things, like Russell taught me. But I did. I stole stuff people was tossin' in the road. Russell yelled at me."

Katina's heart clenched at the sound of Russell's name. *Give me strength!* She said, "Come with us, Bruce. We've all done bad things."

"No."

"Please?"

There was a pause, then slowly, the boy appeared from the darkness, crawling on his hands and knees. Katina took his hand and helped him up. She brushed him off, then took him in a tight hug. He didn't pull away. "We've all done bad things," she said softly around the tears in her voice. "But we've done good things, too, and we are going to survive this. Come with us to the north."

He said nothing, but Katina could feel his head move up and down. *Yes.*

Together, they hurried the distance to the Chicago River.

There was a mob along the river's edge, shoulder to shoulder, and from where she stood on Franklin, Katina could see that all the bridges spanning the water to North Division were swarming with frantic people, their wagons, crates, bundles, and animals. Babies cried in mothers' arms, and fathers shoved to get their families through the swarming mass of bodies. Mules were frozen in place on the river's edge, braying over the shouts and the wind, refusing to move. To the south, the fire was visible over the buildings of the business district, rushing northward in the wind. It could be just minutes before an arm of it reached the river to burn those who waited there and to jump across the water to the North Side.

"We got to cross!" yelled Alice. "We got to get to a bridge!"

"We won't make it," Katina shouted. Inside the satchel, the kitten struggled, sticking its nose out from beneath the flap but unable to escape. "People can barely move on the bridge. Look! They are piled atop each other!"

The river was crowded with boats making for the lake. They were jammed up, waiting for the bridges to turn and let them out. Several boats were burning, and their crews had jumped into the river, clutching anything they could find that would float.

Katina pushed through the people, beckoning the others to follow. She found a pile of shattered furniture, destroyed when the owners had thrown it from an overhead apartment window. "We won't make the bridge! Get in the river with this!"

People near her stared as though she were crazy, but others saw the wisdom of her words, and, dropping what they were carrying, snatched up posts and planks. Katina and Alice lifted the heavy headboard of what had been a mahogany bed, and Bruce and Madame Jocelyn each took a bedpost.

At the river's edge, they watched as some of the brave people slipped down the retaining wall into the water.

*Russell*, Katina thought. *God bless you and keep you. Thank you for your love, courage, and compassion. May I carry on your legacy.*

She broke into sobs as she followed Alice, Madame Jocelyn, and Bruce into the water.

# 20

Russell was struck on the back by a burning post and knocked down. He bucked violently, knocking the post away. Red-hot beams were piled around him and over him, rippling and crawling with the heat as if a million glowing slugs clung to their surfaces. But none were directly on him, as some of the beams had snagged on each other and were held at an angle three feet over his head, forming a small space in which he lay. Russell's clothes, still wet from the river, kept the rest of his body from burning, but the clothes began to smoke.

*Get out get out get out!*

His foot was trapped beneath Ardie, and he kicked at the man. The thug was clearly dead, his torso crushed and his hair beginning to burn.

*Get out!*

Russell jerked his leg free and yanked his coat over his head as best he could. Then, without letting himself think about it because if he did he would have hesitated, he shoved himself as hard as he could, rolling out of the space that protected him and through a solid wall of fire. It felt as though the skin of one side of his face was splitting in the heat. He screamed as one of his hands burned and blistered. But suddenly, he realized he was out of the wreckage, clear of the collapsed building and out in the open.

He rolled over and over, with his hands and face tucked, extinguishing the fire in the dust of Quincy Street. The nerves of his burned hand screamed, a pulsing, terrible rhythm that cut clear to his gut. The side of his face felt as if it had been skinned alive, but he could still see. Near him, a team of firefighters were quitting. The men shouted to each other as they rapidly rolled their charred hose onto the fire truck. Some of their uniforms were smoking from close contact with the intense heat. One man had thrown his broad-brimmed hat to the road, and it lay there in flames. Red embers continued to fall from above.

Russell staggered to his feet. He could still stand.

He could still walk.

The wreckage of the bakery crossed the entire entrance to Rat's Alley, and he would not be able to get back through. He had to make it by another way to the Chicago River, where he prayed Katina had gone. Perhaps John Brandermill had shot her and Madame Jocelyn. Tears sprang to his eyes.

He could still cry.

A fireman saw Russell swaying on his feet, waved his hand, and cried, "Come on now, sir! We're leaving!" As the fire engine's horses stomped, impatient to be clear of the holocaust, and as the fire leaped overhead, Russell limped to the steam engine, where he was hoisted up to stand beside the two firemen on the back runner. "Hold tight!" one fireman shouted to Russell. "We're heading north!"

Russell nodded. God willing, Katina was north.

With a clanging and belching of steam, the engine clattered up Quincy to Market and turned north. Here, the crowds were thick and panicked, screaming, running, pushing each other out of the way for the firemen.

*The world is burning*, Russell thought. *Maybe it's the end of everything. No, not yet. Not till we are together one last time.*

Russell held on to the rail behind the boiler as tightly as he could with one good hand. He was in agony from the burns to his face. Even his chest and legs had been singed through the wet clothes.

"You headin' for the river?" the fireman beside Russell yelled.

Russell nodded.

"Our hose is burned up, can't use it," shouted the fireman. "Our station is a block from the river."

Russell nodded. He closed his eyes, locked his fingers, and let hell roll past. There was an explosion somewhere nearby, and the fireman said, "I bet that's the gasworks!"

In what seemed like seconds, the fireman was nudging him. "Off you go! This is Lake Street. Hop quickly now, we've got to repair before we're at it again."

Russell opened his eyes. "God bless you," he said.

Gentlemen and ladies from the business section of town were on the street and sidewalks, looking less than elegant now. They wore the same fear in their eyes as any other person, rich or poor, and they pushed just as hard to get where they needed to go. Russell let the crowd usher him to the river's edge, where he stared at the broad spectrum of a city in torment. On his side of the river, people struggled with everything they owned toward the bridges; on the other, spectators stared back across the water, transfixed. In the water floated burning boats and people clinging to scrap wood.

How could he find Katina in all of this?

*Let her be safe!*

"We're going to die, aren't we?" asked a gentleman next to Russell. He was well dressed, with a vest, pocket watch chain, and tailored linen jacket and trousers. He was leaning on a broken wooden door that he'd propped up beside himself. "I will. I can't get to the bridge, and if I could I couldn't make it across."

It hurt Russell to speak. "Because the bridge is too crowded?"

"No," said the man. "It's my leg. It's broken, badly, shattered in two places. I fell through a sidewalk, and it snapped like a stick."

"Terrible," was all Russell could offer. His throat was raw and scorched.

"Indeed," replied the gentleman. "I came out of my office and was nearly trampled. Then I broke my leg. I hopped awhile, then found the only crutch I could. This broken door." He smiled a little, as if embarrassed to not have a proper crutch.

"I can't help you walk," said Russell. "My hand's burned and useless. But we can get in the river on your door."

"Oh," said the gentleman, glancing around at the fire. "I can't swim!"

"The door will hold us up."

"And if I slip off?"

"I can swim. I've done this before. You're with an expert."

The man looked doubtful, but it was clear from the trembling of his jaw that he was terrified of being left behind, terrified of dying. He nodded. Russell helped him to the edge of the retaining wall beside a wharf. Bracing with his elbow and knees, Russell helped lower the gentleman into the water with the door. Then he slid down himself, grabbed onto the rough wood with his good hand, and the two floated out toward the center of the river. Several bodies drifted by. On a makeshift raft nearby, several men sang a cheerful German song. The wakes of larger boats brushed them aside, and they bobbed on the waves.

They floated, clinging to the door as the fire reached the river's edge, the gentleman too afraid to talk, Russell too weary and in too much pain. Russell paddled against the current of the river so they would not go out into the lake, pushing off of boats that came too close.

They floated.

Sometime in the early morning, the fire leaped the river to North Division, and by daylight, there were no more spectators on the north bank, only burning warehouses and wharves. The curious had fled.

The gentleman at last spoke. "When do you think it will be safe to get out of the river? My leg is numb."

Russell, his throat cracking and dry, said, "Not yet."

"My name is George Rainey," said the gentleman. "I am a reporter with the *Chicago Tribune*. I dare say my office is cinders by now."

"My name is Russell Cosgrove," said Russell. "I am a poor man who has tried in vain for months to raise money for my charitable home for the honest poor near Conley's Patch. I dare say there is nothing left there, either."

They floated for what seemed like many more hours, talking, Russell's legs working mechanically against the current. The sun, shrouded in smoke, moved overhead and down to the west.

At long last, Russell could see the people on the rafts work over to the south bank, and people on the wharves hauling them up. It was nearly dark, and although there were still fires burning on South Division, the worst seemed to be past. Those living in North Division had a long ordeal still ahead of them.

Russell shouted up to several policemen standing on a dock. "Give us a hand!" Lying prone on the wooden platform, one blister-faced officer reached out and grabbed Russell by both arms, sending a shard of pain to his spine. With a grunt and a tug, Russell was hoisted upward. Once on the dock he forced himself to stand, shivering even in the residual heat of the fire, staring at some of the others who had been brought out of the water. Many were coughing, some sitting and shaking. Others were dead, saved from the blaze but drowned in the river.

George Rainey was dragged up to the dock with a lot of groaning, but Russell did not wait to speak to the gentleman again. He would be fine, even with his broken leg. He was alive.

While most of the city was gone.

Russell walked to the end of the dock, stepping over people, trying not to look at the fear in the eyes of the living and the vacancy in the eyes of the dead. To the south, there were still flames leaping above some buildings, while others smoldered. Buildings of all sizes and uses had been reduced to rubble. The stench of devastation hung in the air. A tiny, soot-covered pony ran past, whinnying in terror, its harness singed and flapping.

Russell stood at the dock's end and stared. He touched the red, crisp skin on his face and the curled, damaged fingers of his hand. *So this is where I'm left. And somehow, I must start over. I don't know how. God, is this destiny? How can I even go on?*

His body began to shake with the tears he'd held inside. Every fiber cried out with grief, and he put his face to his hands and wept.

"Russell?"

Russell dropped his hands and looked down at two women seated on the dock beside him. A drenched, white-haired woman was holding a drenched, auburn-haired young woman. The old woman's face was smeared with lip color and rouge. Hooked to the younger woman's elbow was a brocade satchel. Several feet away was another young woman in a torn, frilly dress and a boy with an angry, wet kitten in his arms.

"Russell?" said the old woman.

"Madame Jocelyn?"

"Russell!" Bruce cried, bounding to his side. "We thought you was dead!"

*Katina!*

Russell fell to his knees and scooped Katina into his arms. Her eyes did not open. Her cold, soaked body did not move.

"We thought you was burned alive!" said Bruce.

Russell rubbed Katina's face, her neck. He put his hand to her heart, but felt nothing. "Katina?"

*No! God, not this! Anything but this!*

He put her head in his lap and began to weep.

*Not after all this!*

He squeezed her close, wanting to take her into himself, to never let her go. To have and to hold. He held her tighter. Tighter.

*Anything but this!*

She moved.

Russell's head shot up. She was looking at him with bleary eyes. "Katina!"

"Russell, you're all wet again," she whispered.

"Yes."

"But I thought you hated being in the river."

He laughed. He kissed the top of her head, rocked her, and laughed.

The sound was glorious on the dark and smoky Chicago wind.

# 21

## Chicago Faces Inferno, and in Spite of Devastation, Hope and Charity Reign

At long last prayers were answered, and a torrent of blessed rain arrived late Monday night over the city of Chicago. The majority of the deadly fire was no longer burning by mid-Tuesday. The inferno ravaged an area four miles long and one mile wide. 17,500 buildings are destroyed, seventy-three miles of streets are gone. Close to 300 people have been burned alive, crushed in falling buildings, jumped to their deaths, or drowned. 100,000 have been left homeless. Crosby's Opera House is destroyed, as were the Steward Grand Theatre and the Tribune Building. This issue of the *Tribune* is being printed from a makeshift office in one small shop which did not burn completely to the ground, with scavenged ink and a donated press.

But there is hope in the aftermath, a spirit that rises higher than any smoke or flame ever could.

In the darkest hour of my life, I met a young man, unassuming and brave, named Russell Cosgrove. In the midst of the terrible calamity that has befallen our city, Mr. Cosgrove, despite his own dire injuries, took pity on a stranger, helping him survive a night of hell on the river.

Charity has sprung up in Chicago, with donations pouring in to those devastated by the fire. Yet, I suggest strongly that Mr. Russell Cosgrove be sought out, wherever he is. He chastised my heart without knowing it when he told me simply that he had worked for months, without success, to raise money for the honest poor around Conley's Patch. As a wellspring has been opened in oft-hardened hearts, I pray that those of wealth will take pity on our less fortunate brethren, that they will see them as Mr. Cosgrove sees them, not just during a tragedy but year-round.

For to those who go without, every day can be tragic, indeed.

—George Rainey, *Chicago Tribune*,
October 11, 1871

# 22

# 1891

October had been a particularly rainy month, with chilly breezes sweeping the city. Quincy Street was cobblestoned now, but rainwater still found ways to collect in low spots and send pedestrians to the streetside walkways. Telegraph wires had been joined by telephone wires, crisscrossing Chicago like a vast network of spiderwebs. Electric trolleys had taken the place of the horsecars.

Russell stood at the window of his apartment, looking out at the morning rain as it drenched the neighboring apartment buildings and drizzled down the window glass. He could see his reflection, lit by the gaslight burning over the desk behind him. Tall, dark hair, a trim beard obscuring the scar that had formed on his face from the burn he had suffered long ago. One strong arm, one locked in paralysis.

"I wonder how much longer it's going to rain?" he asked.

The beautiful woman at the desk put down her pen and smiled. Russell turned from the window, letting the curtains fall back into place.

"I remember saying once I never wanted to see another raindrop," said Katina. Her auburn hair, now long and full, was swept up and pinned, with tiny curls at her cheeks. "Now I leave the weather up to itself."

"How is the play coming?"

"Oh," said Katina, glancing at the spread of pages on the desk before her. "This one is difficult, but I think it will be strong when it's finished."

"The audiences at the Steward Grand loved your last play. They've been clamoring for another."

Katina raised one eyebrow. At thirty-eight, she was even more lovely than she was twenty years ago. "I'd always dreamed of fame and fortune," she said with a laugh. "And here it is, with only a fair wage and not a soul recognizing me on the street. Except, of course, the Monroes from Michigan Avenue. Ever since my name has been mentioned in the *Tribune* as a playwright of some notice, they have been happy to invite me to tea regardless of their views on derelict Southerners! It irks me to have to call them cousins!"

Russell kissed the top of her hair. She smelled of love and joy.

The door to the study opened, and a tall, handsome young man with dark hair bounded through the door. "Father!" he said breathlessly. "Bruce and I were opening Homeplace, getting the fire going in the stove and setting out the books for the children's morning lessons, when a gentleman rode up on his horse and handed me this envelope. He directed me to give it to you immediately!"

Russell thanked his son, took the envelope, and opened it. It was another check, drawn on the Bank of Chicago, from George Rainey. Ever since the fire, the man had taken it upon himself to collect donations of goods and cash from his wealthy friends twice a year for Homeplace. A new building had been built on the site where the old Stick Saloon had stood, with rooms for schooling and meals, and even a temporary shelter for women whose husbands were violent. Upstairs from Homeplace was a modest apartment for Russell, Katina, and their eighteen-year-old son.

"Thank you, William," said Russell. "I'll be down in a minute. If the children come in and get rowdy, sing with them. You are always good at keeping order!"

"Yes, sir," said William. He smiled at his mother, and trotted off.

Russell put his hands on Katina's shoulders, then she stood and circled his waist with her arms, putting her face against his chest. "I never understood how that terrible fire could have been destiny," she said softly. "I never could believe that something like that was meant to be. I've since realized that much in life will never make sense, but as long as we see what is in front of us, and appreciate the lessons, the gifts, then we will be blessed."

Russell lifted her chin and looked into her eyes. "You are truly my gift."

Katina kissed him. He held her tightly, never wanting to let go. Then they walked to the window, clinging to each other, warm and safe, and watched the rain and the streets and the distant steeples and towers and the birds circling the air and flying out over the city to the sparkling lake to the east.

# A Note from the Author

*One dark night, when we were all in bed,*
*Lady O'Leary left a lantern in the shed,*
*And when the cow kicked it over, she winked*
    *her eye and said,*
*There'll be a hot time in the old town tonight!*
                    —folk song, author unknown

I've never lived in Chicago, but I have been fascinated with its people and its culture. Some of my best friends are Chicagoans, and they are fiercely loyal to their city and its works—from Lake Shore Drive to the Bulls to the sky-scraping Sears Tower. I was excited by the opportunity to write a book set in the Windy City during one of its most memorable, and devastating, historical events.

In the 1870s Chicago was a city of growth and vision. As a metropolis on the frontier, it seemed just a little rougher and a little wilder than its eastern cousins such as Boston, New York, and Baltimore. It was a bit of modern civilization raised from the swampy land by Lake Michigan—determined, creative, and hardheaded. A town of less than 100 citizens in 1833, Chicago had grown in only thirty-eight years to a city of over 334,000. The citizens were proud of their modern fire alarm network, their trained firefighters, and their up-to-date water system, which pumped water from the lake to hydrants all over town.

What really went wrong on the night of October 8, 1871? Chicago was used to fires; when not battling rain and mud, Chicagoans often endured long stretches of dry weather. The city was windy, and most of it was built of wood. It was not shocking to read in the newspaper of a fire the previous day claiming a home or factory. But how did this one get so dreadfully out of hand? Was someone to blame? Or was it just a terrible accident?

One thing was clear. The fire began in the barn of Catherine and Patrick O'Leary on De Koven Street. But in the 1870s, newspaper articles often read more like modern-day tabloids. Reporters didn't always check the sources of their information, and sometimes even made up whole stories. While the fire did start at the O'Learys', it was reported by the Chicago *Evening Journal* that the O'Leary cow kicked over a lamp while Mrs. O'Leary was milking. The Chicago *Times* said that Mrs. O'Leary was an "old hag" of about seventy years who had set the fire on purpose because she was no longer allowed to get county relief (an assistance to the poor) and wanted revenge against the city. None of this was true. Mrs. O'Leary was only in her thirties, had never been on county relief, and had been in bed asleep when the fire began. However, the newspapers had given the city someone to blame, and the woman suffered for it the rest of her life. Cartoons were drawn, showing a witch-like Catherine milking her cow. Hordes of the curious came to their burned-down home to stare. A postcard was even made and sold, showing a haggard old woman, posed as Catherine, with a cow and a milk pail.

While to this day Catherine O'Leary is unjustly infamous for starting the fire, there were other curious accusations. Some rumors blamed "Peg Leg" Sullivan for setting the fire while drinking. There was even gossip that a fire extinguisher salesman, despondent because of poor sales, set the fire to show why his product was needed.

But why did the fire spread so quickly with so little resistance? Again, people wanted a scapegoat. Some accused firefighters of being drunk that night. Even the poor of the city had blame placed on them, with accusations that immigrants had slowed the progress of the firefighters by drifting along in the streets, disorderly, rioting and cursing.

An inquiry was held in Chicago in November. Many solid reasons were offered as to the reason the city burned. These included the very dry weather, the strong wind, and the fact that so much wood was used in the construction of houses, sidewalks, businesses, and roads. It was also pointed out that the fire department did not have enough men on staff, that an alarm was not turned in at Goll's drugstore, that there were not enough hydrants, and there was a lack of fireboats to patrol the river.

New building regulations were put into place after the Great Fire. Unfortunately, they required most of the buildings that had been destroyed to be rebuilt with stone or brick. Because most of the poor did not have fire insurance, they could not afford to do this. The division between rich and poor grew wider as those without the means to build according to code were forced to rebuild their new, wood homes outside the city's commercial district. Justice-minded people like my fictional Russell Cosgrove and Katina Monroe would have had to continue working hard to bring awareness of the plight of the poor to the wealthy.

To find out more about Chicago and the fire, I suggest reading *The Great Fire* by Jim Murphy and *Chicago: Growth of a Metropolis* by Harold M. Mayer and Richard C. Wade.

# About the Author

ELIZABETH MASSIE is a native Virginian who lives in the beautiful Shenandoah Valley. She writes all kinds of fiction: historicals, suspense, mainstream, and even picture books. She has authored several adult novels: *Sineater, Welcome Back to the Night,* and *Dark Shadows: Dreams of the Dark* (co-written with Stephen Mark Rainey). Her work for young adults includes *Buffy the Vampire Slayer: Power of Persuasion* and the upcoming series *Young Founders.* For middle-grade readers, she has written the *Daughters of Liberty* trilogy. For little guys she co-authored *Jambo, Watoto!* with her sister, Barbara Spilman Lawson.

Besides writing, Elizabeth enjoys reading, camping, and traveling. Favorite movies include *It's a Mad Mad Mad Mad World* and *Life Is Beautiful.* Her favorite book is *To Kill a Mockingbird.* She is the mother of two wonderful young adults, Erin and Brian. She has performed in local theater, and in her spare time picks ticks off her dog Sandy and watches late-night reruns of *Law and Order.* You can write her at iritgud@cfw.com